FUGITIVE

for Tanya

David Butler

FUGITIVE

ARLEN
HOUSE

Fugitive

is published in 2021 by
ARLEN HOUSE
42 Grange Abbey Road
Baldoyle, Dublin 13, Ireland
Phone: 00 353 86 8360236
arlenhouse@gmail.com
arlenhouse.blogspot.com

978–1–85132–228–2, *paperback*

Distributed internationally by
SYRACUSE UNIVERSITY PRESS
621 Skytop Road, Suite 110
Syracuse, NY 13244–5290
Phone: 315–443–5534
Fax: 315–443–5545
supress@syr.edu
syracuseuniversitypress.syr.edu

Typesetting by Arlen House

cover image:
'Death : Rebirth'
by Amy Flaherty
is reproduced courtesy of the artist

CONTENTS

My thanks to Tanya, who has suffered many a first draft; to the Brooks Writers – Joanne Hayden, June Caldwell, Lisa Harding, Liz McSkeane, Henry McDonald, Julie Cruickshank, Ger Moane, Manus Boyle, Aiden O'Reilly – for their attention and advice; to Danielle McLaughlin, Billy O'Callaghan and Mary O'Donnell for their generous comments on the manuscript; to my extended family for their continued support; and to publisher Alan Hayes, whose energy and persistence are legendary.

The stories collected here won the Benedict Kiely, Maria Edgeworth, ITT/Redline and Fish International awards, and were placed or shortlisted for the Francis MacManus, Colm Tóibín, Benedict Kiely, James Plunkett, H.E. Bates, Aesthetica, Walter Scott, *Writers' & Artists' Yearbook*, *London Magazine*, Wild Atlantic Way, Bath, Exeter, Cambridge TSS, Words by Water, Words on the Water, Retreat West, From the Well, People's College, Pin Drop and Loft Books competitions. They have featured on the longlist for the Irish Short Story of the Year in 2017, 2018, 2019, 2020 and 2021, and have been translated into several European languages.

The stories have been published in the *Stinging Fly*, the *Lonely Crowd*, *Crannóg*, the *Blue Nib*, the *Amsterdam Quarterly*, the *Manchester Review*, *Ofi*, *Libartes*, *Inrocki*, *Circle Show* (US), *Retreat West*, and the *Aesthetica, Bath, Fish, Redline* and *From the Well* anthologies.

APHASIA

'The trauma is here,' the neurologist says, 'you see?' Her biro is tracing a circle about a darkened area to one side of the monitor. A Rorschach test, say. A walnut, infinite space bounded in a nutshell. I'm here at the mother's request. Rajid is my student.

'So what does it mean?'

'It's early to say. With trauma to the frontal lobe there may be some loss of movement. Down the right hand side.'

'Bloody racists!' says the father.

'Also,' she lays down the biro, nods slowly, 'there may be impairment to the speech function.'

'Bloody racists!' Mr Shafiq is a small, ferocious man with a potbelly. It's his fourth time to say it. His wife, the dentist, has a deep thumbprint of insomnia beneath each eye. She asks 'in what way, his speech function?'

'He may have difficulty with sentence structure. Forming sentences.' The doctor rubs her left temple, is explaining something or other about the Broca area. But I'm picturing the last time I spoke with Rajid; a good-looking lad, raven haired, a flash of white teeth. Impossible to square that image with the damaged moth flickering on the screen. Though I too am well acquainted with the devastation of brain trauma. My cousin, Andrew. For twenty years Aunt Mary has fed him baby food with a plastic spoon; Uncle John silent, stern, reading it as divine judgement.

The word *aphasia* pulls me back to the present. 'With this kind of aphasia, the patient is very often aware of their condition and can become intensely frustrated. *Everyone* will need to be patient.' She directs *everyone* toward Mr Shafiq.

Before we leave I look in on him again, lying as though asleep on the gurney, so vulnerable in the thin hospital gown. Once I've waved off the Shafiqs' taxi, I return to have a brief word with the Garda. Is there a chance of charging anyone over the attack?

'In this town? See no evil, speak no evil is the motto here.' The best hope, she implies though shaking her head, is if, afterwards, the victim can give us some kind of a description. Afterwards.

I'm filled with anxiety flutters. They're something I've become increasingly prone to. Hard to believe the skull, that cage of infinity, can be so fragile. A single boot to the head had done the real damage. On a whim I walk out as far as the People's Park; allow my thoughts space to wander. *Trauma* from the Greek, a hurt or a wound. Though *Traum* in German means dream. I've heard it said the amputee dreams he is whole, that each waking is a new amputation. What dream will Rajid wake from? And wake into? Or my cousin Andrew for that matter?

The police tape is gone from the bushes where the attack took place. On Friday evening, about half past eight. It wasn't even dark. Today is Sunday, and the low clouds and hint of rain have the place half empty. All the same, even with rain imminent, there are still people about. A man and dog over by the footbridge; a woman with a pushchair; a couple of teens bent like streetlights over their iPhones. Impossible to think no one witnessed the attack.

See no evil, speak no evil.

Looking up, a line from one of Rajid's stories comes to me: *The sky was pregnant with rain, and before we got home the waters broke.* That's how he was; witty. A witty individual. Something of an all-rounder, too. He played cricket and was a winger on the college soccer team.

What was it brought him out here, to this place?

A memory, something I'd seen and shouldn't have seen, grips me. Rajid and Danny Keane behind the bike shed. My office overlooks it. I'd assumed they'd gone there for a sneaky fag – you weren't supposed to smoke if you were on the soccer team. What I saw wasn't a kiss, not quite. Not technically. But Danny's hand took the back of Rajid's neck with exquisite tenderness and drew their heads together. Together they rested, perhaps a minute, then with a pat to the cheek they broke. Would he know what had brought his teammate out here? Padma Shafiq has her dental practice out the Dublin Road, that much I know already. Where Danny Keane lives I can find out handy enough – the dad runs a call-out plumbing business.

The address turns out to be in one of the older council estates, not squalid but somehow passed over. Nothing much has changed here since the seventies, except that satellite dishes have replaced the Chinese script of TV aerials. Pebbledash and concrete, brambles of graffiti, a few boarded-up windows. On the green a burned-out car, orange with rust, with an enormous sofa disembowelled beside it. The Keane house is toward the far end of the innermost terrace, the number I'd jotted down confirmed by the plumber's van parked outside. As I walk toward it, I feel the weight of the anonymous houses watching me.

The front door is answered by a woman in a housecoat. I can hear the thrum of a mower out the back. 'Would Danny be in?'

An emotion, not quite fear, passes over her face. 'Trevor! Fella here is looking to talk to Danny!' The kitchen door opens and into the hall steps Trevor Keane in shirtsleeves. He replaces his missus at the door, a big man with a high complexion. We have a nodding acquaintance from the football field. 'I was hoping to have a word with Danny,' I say.

'With Danny, is it? Dan doesn't do any of your subjects.' He shifts, as if caught out on a lie. 'Anyway, he's not here.'

'I expect you've heard Rajid Shafiq was set upon Friday evening.' No answer. 'Yes?' He shakes his head, as if he hasn't quite understood me. 'I was at the hospital to see him earlier on.' His face is glazed over. 'He's in a very bad way.'

'What's any of this got to do with Danny?'

'I just thought he might know what Rajid was up to on Friday evening. Who he was with. Why he was in the park ...'

The sound of the lawnmower dying diverts both of our attentions. He makes a grimace, an exaggeration of dumbness, and says 'nah.' Then he breathes in and adds 'I told you already. He's not here' and makes to shut the door, but my foot prevents it. His pale eyes are indignant. 'I just need two minutes,' I bid, 'ok?' Before he has the chance to shove the door shut, Danny, in grass-stained tracksuit, appears in the kitchen. There is a jolt when he sees me; a rigidity. In that instant I know that he knows why I'm here.

Over the man's shoulder, I wave. Danny is awkward, unsure whether or how to respond. 'Go upstairs, Dan.' He doesn't look at his son, he looks directly at me. Unwilling to put the boy in an impossible position, I wait until Danny has gone upstairs before continuing. 'Mr Keane, I just need to talk to him for two minutes is all.'

'I don't think so.'

'He might know,' I shrug, 'something. Anything. The guards have said that no matter how insignificant ...'

'Look. Danny didn't see anything. Danny didn't hear anything. Right? You,' a finger, nicotine yellow, pokes my collarbone, 'leave our boy alone.'

I turn but I remain at the threshold, not yet ready to abandon the hunch I'm working off. 'Let me tell you about brain trauma,' I say. I tell him how my cousin has spent the last twenty years, twisted like a question mark in a wheelchair. 'His life over,' I snap my fingers, 'like that.' He is waiting for me to finish. 'At least that was an accident. He came off a motorbike. But *this*?'

He says something then that takes a second to register. 'You never got married.' There is unguarded loathing pushing up his blood pressure. 'Why is that?'

I guffaw 'I'm sorry?' But the door has snapped shut on my astonishment. The house is imperturbable but for a twitch behind the curtain upstairs. A couple of minutes later, as I walk away, the father's voice overtakes me. 'Tough break, your cousin.'

Back in the park, at the footbridge, I'm as jittery as if I've had a thousand coffees. Because there must have been things said in that house. Words exchanged. Maybe even slaps. The first, ugly thought, that it was Trevor Keane who'd landed the boot to the side of Rajid's skull, has gone. Too fantastic. Too ...

But there was something *not* being said. Suppose Danny had been with Rajid at the time he was set upon. Suppose he'd left him. Abandoned him. Turned on him. Suppose he knew who'd been behind the attack, and what had motivated it. Should I now go to the guards? Tip them off?

Still I remain, watching the slow flow of the river. Because when it comes to it, what do I know? A gesture half seen. The wordless menace after a domestic row. A twitch of a curtain. I think of Rajid, lying on the gurney in the thin hospital gown, of the months and years ahead of him. And I think of Andrew, the kiss he pressed on me the night of the crash, and all that I never said to him.

Taylor Keith

The mist rolling off the mountain was threatening rain, otherwise we'd never have taken that lift. The van hissed past us, slow enough to see your man eyeing us from under his farmer's cap, but steady, like he'd no thought of stopping. I didn't even turn to watch the van get small, just dropped the cardboard sign – *oh please* – Sharon had done with her lipstick. The rain was starting to fall in fat drops. Then over my shoulder came the crunch. It's a sound you'd pick out on the busiest of roads. Then silence, like a question mark.

He'd pulled over this side of the stone bridge. After a couple of seconds, the indicator started to wink. But I'm telling you there was something about that Hiace. I fired a look at Sharon as much as to say so. She shrugged, not smiling, but kind of 'what the hell?' Besides, she'd already flung her bag over her shoulder. So there was nothing for it. We ran that hundred yards in case your man changed his mind. Or in case it was a prank. Some jokers do that, let you get all the way up to the door before they pull away.

You can smell the funny ones a mile off. But what are you going to do? They've pulled over, you've run up to them, you're hardly going to say *oh, I thought it was someone else like* ... Still I could nearly have scripted it, when I pulled the door after me and seen what Sharon was sitting in beside. The hair, where it jutted out from under the cap, was dyed the colour of red lemonade. Eyebrows, too. I say dyed, but maybe not, the sideburns were grey enough. Might've been anywhere in his forties, fifties, or sixties, it's impossible to tell with these farmer types. The big roundy head on him.

Next thing I notice, after I get over the hum of stale piss and cabbage, is a string of rosary beads that's set slapping against the windscreen the moment we jerk out onto the road. They're wrapped a couple of turns around the mirror, with three big miraculous medals dangling off like charms from a bracelet. Himself fires a knowing look, like they're nothing at all to do with him! Then there's this crunch of gears you wouldn't believe, as if head-the-ball isn't at all used to driving. I feel Shazzer's elbow dig into me as she sings out: 'you're a life-saver mister, we're stuck on that mountain this last hour so we are.' Instead of asking him how far he was going, like. Our friend seems to be in no hurry to say anything at all, just tilts the cap and narrows the eye, as much as to say *I'm a real cute hoor*. The midlands, I swear to god. But in any case, the heavens pick that moment to open, and the rain drumming on the roof is that loud we'd have to shout to hear one another. Naturally there's only the one wiper that works, and for the next twenty minutes it's like we're driving through a mirage of the midlands. The mercy of god there's only Sunday traffic about.

Now, things haven't been going any too well between myself and Sharon. It was yours truly had cajoled her to get away for the weekend, a break from her studies like. But, of course, my agenda was to get the old flame going again. Fat chance of that, with the lack of funds. Slept rough the last night, we did. Under the real Irish weather, too, and bollox all to eat in the morning let alone smoke. So she's dead keen to get back to Galway. Told me her exams is starting tomorrow, though I'd swear she said earlier they weren't till Thursday. It's now bucketing down like we're inside of a carwash. Maybe that's why she hasn't asked our friend how far he's going. Fear it'd remind him to turn off, for his farm.

Then, without a word, he does pull over. Small little place, a couple of shops, a pub. Biggest thing in it is the road. The rain has started to ease off, anyhow. 'Are ye hungry?' he asks. I'm thinking, we're broke as a joke, let's just squeeze a few more miles out of this guy, but not Shazzer. 'Starving!' she smiles, straight at him. You want to see what that girl can do with a smile! 'Come on, so.' And before I have a chance to tug at her anorak, she's followed him down out of the driver's door. So that's that, we trot across as far as the café.

'I suppose,' says he, before we go in, 'yez have no money, aye.' We look at one another and nod back at his nod. 'Have a good feed for yourselves,' he goes, tapping the wallet in his pocket, 'I've a little business to attend to.' There must be some law down the country that you can't say the word 'business' without winking.

'How exactly are we going to pay for any of this, Shaz?' The two of us are sitting by the window, the way we can keep an eye on the van. Just in case, d'you know? Shazzer's after ordering the full Irish. With chips, if you don't mind. There's only the one woman in the place, waitress, cashier and cook all rolled into one. Mouth on her like a sphincter. For the time being, while she's in the kitchen, we're on our own. 'You're such a ...' Sharon goes, pulling a face.

'What if he doesn't come back?'

'He's coming back.'

'All I'm saying, what if he *doesn't* come back?'

She just shakes her hair at me, so it flicks either side of her mouth. I swear, it kills me every time. So anyway, I've long since wiped up the last baked bean with my single slice of toast and she's making a big deal out of the full Irish when in walks *mo dhuine*. He throws a sly glance to the counter – your one is out the back somewhere – saunters over to us, puts a hand on Sharon's shoulder, and leans in. 'I don't know about you people,' says he, 'but I'm doing a runner.' And with a dirty wink, he's gone, setting the doorbell tinkling. 'What the ...' For a second, we're paralysed. Then the two of us are literally falling over one another to get the hell out of the place.

As the van judders out onto the road Shazzer is laughing like she's gone crazy. It's not fear, it's pure adrenalin man. She's loving it. 'Jesus Christ!' I cry, still struggling to get the door shut 'that was some stunt you pulled my friend!' Himself, of course, says nothing for another country mile, just the same cute hoor squint. The stink of piss or cabbage is laced over with something sweet, diesel maybe. I suppose that was his 'bit of business (wink)'. Then he goes to Sharon, like maybe five minutes later 'and had you a good feed itself?' I stay shtum. I'm spitting feathers because after a long weekend of sulks and tantrums, Sharon Donlon has suddenly turned on the girly charm for Bilbo fucking Baggins. His eyes meet mine in the mirror and they stay there so long I can't see how we haven't wound up in the ditch. 'What?' I snap. 'What?' 'I just wanted to see,' says he, 'what yez are made of is all.' And then, after another country mile 'I knew well you'd be game.' We're driving along a stretch of road that's somehow familiar. Those sheep. That mountain. I see his hand grip Sharon's knee and give it a little squeeze. 'I'm seldom mishtaken.'

16

Shazzer throws me a glance. For the first time, she's maybe nervous. 'Game for what?' she goes, just as we're trundling over the very bridge where I'd swear he'd first picked us up. This time, he makes to go right at the T-junction. 'Pull over!' I shout. 'Pull the van over pal, right fucking now.'

He does so. Even before it's come to a stop I've the door open. 'You want to tell us what the fuck stunt you've been pulling, driving us around in circles?' He looks at me in the mirror. Big, dirty eyes on him, and the orange eyebrows hoisted high. 'Sure yez never told me where you wanted to get to.' 'Galway,' mutters Sharon. Her head is angled forwards. The chain I gave her for her twenty first is in her mouth, a fine silver bridle. She's starting not to like this one little bit.

'Galway, bedad!' He rubs his big ear between finger and thumb as though it aids the calculation. 'That's a good hundred mile.' 'I've to get back, for exams,' says Sharon, quietly. Her mood has changed right enough. Our friend pushes the cap far back on his head and scratches the orange hairline. 'How would you like to get back to Galway,' says he, 'all in one go?' Sharon is gazing hard at the dashboard, so he looks steadily past her at me. 'Can ayther of you drive?'

I shake my head. 'What's driving got to do with it?'

Sharon sits up, stares at the man. 'I can drive!' she goes. Then she flashes her eyes at me, as though I'd dare contradict her. 'I can!' she repeats, brightly. She can in her hole. 'Can you, now,' says our friend, and the next thing, he has the door open, and he skips out onto the road. 'Well that's settled then.'

'Settled! What's settled?'

'Take her. Far as Galway.'

'Your ... *van*?'

He slaps the driver's seat, and when he removes his palm there's twenty quid on it. 'That'll cover any diesel, get yez a pint once ye get there.' He straightens his cap, fires another trademark wink. 'She's not my van.' And then he shuts over the door and sets off at a good clip down the road. I think I can say we're too dumbstruck to move. We just look at one another, then at the shabby dashboard with its rosary and miniature statue. Suddenly I stick my head out and shout after him. 'What are we supposed to do with the van, once we get there?'

He doesn't even turn. He just holds up a hand, as though he's waving back to us. 'I was you fellas,' he calls, 'I'd put a match to her.'

To this day I marvel that we ever got there. Shazzer could no more drive than I could. It took her three attempts just to get the bloody Hiace to move without juddering to a halt ten yards along the road. Every junction, every roundabout, was a disaster waiting to happen. To make matters worse it was well after dark again we got over the Shannon, and, of course, the van had only the one dim headlight. I swear, there mustn't have been a single guard out that Sunday or we'd've been pulled over. Four hours it took us. A hundred miles, not even. The only bonus, we never had to stop for that diesel.

It was only once we'd passed Athenry that we began to talk about where to dump it. I said we should just abandon ship, walk or thumb the last couple of mile. But herself was having none of it. Too simple by half. 'It'll have to be burnt,' she goes. 'Fingerprints.' I suppose she had a point. *Maybe.*

'Bright side,' says I, chancing an arm around her shoulder, 'at least there's no shortage of wasteland around Galway to set a bonfire.' I was desperate to get her to move back to Dublin, even if it was only for the summer. 'Or torch a van,' says she, head almost glued to the windscreen to see out into the night.

We swung into an industrial wasteland somewhere near Oranmore I think it was. Old abandoned plant, all the windows broke. Everything weeded over. Strange as it may sound, we'd barely said a word about you know who, and what he might've been up to. Taylor Keith, Shazzer called him. On account of the hair. I guess she was happy to be this near home, twenty quid in her arse pocket and an adventure to be laughed over with her flatmates. I was glad just to be hanging around her now she was back on a high.

I don't know if you've ever tried to light diesel. It doesn't fucking burn. It takes me three or four goes to find that out, dropping a bit of rolled up newspaper lit like a torch into the tank. Waiting for the thump, like you'd hear on telly. Nothing. Of course herself is now acting like she knew that all along, and I'm a prize eejit. And then I remember, that funny sweet smell inside of the van, above the piss and the cabbage. With the tank screwed open, I know it wasn't diesel. Maybe, while we were in that café, our old pal Taylor Keith threw a can of petrol into the back. Wasn't there every likelihood he'd planned to do the job himself, only he chanced upon two gobshites to do it for him?

And then it comes to me, like a blow to the solar plexus. We've never even thought about what else might be in the back of that van!

It isn't long to find out. The minute I yank at the handle the door bursts open, as though there's a great weight leaned against it. And sure enough there is. It half slumps, half tumbles out, hitting my thigh hard. Though the bulk of it still lies inside. 'Fuck!' I cry out, skipping away. There, swinging low over the tow bar, is a great grinning horse's mouth, teeth like piano keys. They're propped apart to one side by an enormous rubber tongue. The neck, long and twisted through an impossible angle, is black and white, the way you do get on a cow. 'Jesus *fucking* Christ!'

'Huh!' says Sharon. She's staring at the dead horse, her head nodding up and down, her eyes kind of glazed over.

'We should go to the guards, Shaz, this is fucked up.'

But, of course, we didn't go to the guards. We should've gone to the guards, but we didn't. What can I tell you? Turns out, there was a can of petrol stashed in the back. But whether it was because my hands were so full of the shakes by this stage, or because I was trying to rush things for fear of getting caught, I must've managed to splash my trousers. No sooner had I thrown a match into the back of the van than there was a rush of blue flame down the horse's neck that caught the ends of them, and to cut a long and agonising story short, by the time we'd got my pants off me, I'd burns to both legs. Hands, too. Nothing too horrific, but needing hospital all the same. And it didn't take the guards long to put two and two together, seeing it was in Oranmore we flagged down a passing car. The last thing I remember, as I limped trouserless on Sharon's shoulder, was the roar of orange reflected in a thousand broken black puddles all about that abandoned factory.

I suppose we got off light enough. Neither of us had to do time. But we never hung out after that, Shazzer dropping out of college and all. And I for one haven't ventured my thumb on a road since that wet day.

We'd tried, of course, to explain to the guards that it was Taylor Keith had done in that tinkers' horse, and stole their van on them. By Jaysus, he was some cute hoor all the same. Both of us had been positively identified by sphincter lips doing a runner from her café and speeding off in the same dirty Hiace. She never saw any farmer next or near us. How do you explain that? And *what* colour did you say your man's hair was?

TOO COLD FOR SNOW

I've slept badly again. The farmhouse is unearthly cold. Alive, too, in the still of night, with ticks, groans, intestinal gurgles. The fridge juddering to a halt.

Alice was restless. Shy of dawn I heard her get up, potter about downstairs. She's left a note on the kitchen table: *can run you into the village in the afternoon.* Ok, maybe. I'll have to check texts at *some* point. Go through with the renewal. Let Leonora know I won't be picking Jen up Saturday after all. But it's good to be out here, with neither wifi nor mobile coverage. Alice doesn't even have a TV for god's sake, just an old Telefunken on which she plays vinyls, and a CD player she keeps down the studio. I hug the duvet about my shoulders, shuffle to the stove, touch the cafetière with the back of my hand. It's tepid, meaning she's gone, what? A quarter of an hour?

No microwave. Really, she's taking this back-to-nature lark a bit far. But that's Alice all over. Post-divorce Alice. I tip the remainder of the coffee into a saucepan and spark the gas. On the fifth click it takes, gurgles into a corona of blue buds. Last night I'd blackened the stems of our cigarettes taking a light from one. Curious, she won't let either one of us smoke indoors, when she's twice the smoker that ever I was. Alright sweet Alice, where d'you keep your fags?

The yard is frigid. Frost has turned the mountains to quartz. I draw on the crooked butt – all I could find – and hold in the smoke until I'm dizzy for want of air, then let the air rush like liquid into my lungs. Tincture of manure, despite the freeze. An anxious rush. *Don't think! Not yet.* I flick the spent fag end across the cobbles to where we'd sat out, shivering; where one wine glass remains, cupping an opaque doily of ice. We'd measured time by Orion inching over the gable. A week here would be just the thing. Sneak back incognito. A new man, if I can only beat this insomnia. Calm these jitters.

I hug the duvet tighter about me. I've no wish to go back inside just yet. The interior is gloomy; that's one disadvantage of these old farmhouses. Only her studio is bright, and that cost a small fortune by all accounts. Seeing a scatter of paw prints by the gate, a fancy comes to me that I might be able to track them: the yard is dusted with frost, and the fields are white-haired. They can't have gone that far. If I'd my boots on I'd have a go. But through my socks the bones of my feet are aching.

Alice married at twenty three, and I've never forgiven her. She's seven years older than me. She'd felt she had to look out for us, father becoming so incapable after mother's long cancer. Or perhaps she was simply tired of running wild. Afraid of it, who knows? In those days, I'd idolized her. Several times while still at art college she'd woken up in casualty. One temple still shows a silver bite of scar tissue where she'd fallen on a glass. Was it that stunt that made her see sense? One way or another, when she began to do a line with Donal Walsh, with teetotal Donal of the Traffic Corps, I knew she'd already made up her mind. A wild fowl that's let its flight feathers be drawn. She even developed a waddle, stopped dyeing her hair blues and purples. I never forgave her, and she's always known it.

But who can tell what way a life will pan out? After the cot death she hit the bottle. Not hard, but steadily. Deliberately. In the end, even Sgt Walsh had enough, sought solace in a paramedic who was raising two kids of her own. And Alice couldn't have cared less. All of which at least made for an amicable settlement. No surviving children to bring their antipathies into focus. Now here she is at forty four, a recluse, imperturbable, hair streaked with silver, finally living her idea of being an artist. Still carrying the residue of that cot death.

I'm alerted by a nose nuzzling my palm. Not long after she bought the place Alice recovered the dog from a pet refuge, called it Fred, for all that it's a collie bitch. A nervous animal, shy of people. The nose is a sign she's getting used to me, now I've slept over. Alice isn't far behind, her face hidden in a huge muffler that takes a few seconds to unravel. Breath like candyfloss in the gelid air. 'You might have put some clothes on, mister.'

'Expecting company?' The quip is out before I think she might hear a barb in it. If she has, she doesn't let on. 'So?' she says, pulling at her boots.

'So?'

'Come to any decision?'

Stab of angst. 'I think I might hang on a few more days.' I make to scratch behind Fred's ear, but she cowers away.

'Gerry, you'll have to face the music at some point.'

'I know that. All I'm saying, I could use a few more days.' Fred has sidled behind her and is watching me with distrust. 'If it's all the same to you ...'

Sure, she shrugs, hand on the doorjamb, one boot stubborn. Then she's peering in through the doorway. 'You get a smell of burn?'

'Jesus, the coffee!'

She's been gone twenty minutes, the dog having jumped into the 4x4 beside her. Seeing I've decided to stay on, she's decided we need to stock up. Besides, she informed Fred, the radio says we're in for snow.

'Snow.' I scratched at my stubble. *'Really?'*

'You'd be surprised. Old Taffe says half the county was cut off for a week up here the year of the big freeze. Sure you won't come? Check your car?'

'Nah, I'm good. They said it might be a couple of days before they got the parts.' Then she asked did I want the paper. A knowing look. No TV, and with the radio down in her studio we've had precious little news beyond headlines. I shrugged ok. May as well know the worst, hey?

I'd let out the story, in dribs and drabs, the previous night. The edited version. Alice wasn't drinking, or no more than the one glass of wine. No interest in it, since her long flirtation with spirits came to a halt. All the same the second bottle was her idea. Surrounded by stillness, by the frost-hardened night, it seemed possible to be ... what? Truthful? Intimate? Because we'd never had such a talk, not in twenty years.

I'd expected her to give me a harder time. Ten years ago she would have. Donal Walsh had had to dig me out, once, when it looked like I'd be done for drink driving. Pulled a few favours. I was twenty six; had finally landed a steady job. On that occasion she'd read me the riot act. She was pregnant, and Donal was just getting on in the force, so she'd every right to. Now, under the slow wheel of constellations, she was more the counsellor or therapist. 'Gerry, I'm not your mother.' No Alice, you're not.

She did suggest I have a long word with Donal. Not involve him, as such. But he'd been twenty years on the force, be stupid not to tap into that experience. After all, at one level it *was* a traffic offence. 'You really don't think he'd mind?' She didn't answer. Paused for effect, rather, eyebrows hoisted. I should have asked, would *she* mind. 'Alice, he thinks I'm a plonker.'

'You are a plonker!'

I guffawed, and let it go at that. Time enough.

Soon after she drove off, the landline erupted, rang a ridiculous length through the empty house. It stopped, waited, then repeated the performance. Now, a watchful silence has returned. I set down the pot with its spiral of suds speckled with black. She'd said not to bother, but hell. Thought I might surprise her.

I give the pot a rinse, dribble the whorl of suds over the drain; a thumbprint; an entire galaxy. A track of specks still clings to the scoured aluminium. 'God's sake, leave it, Ger,' she'd sighed. 'It'll do me to clean my brushes.' So be it! Down with it to the studio, which is never locked. There's still frost in the shadowed parts that day hasn't reached; along the foot of the wall, under the hedgerows. Its blue-whiteness reverses Wicklow to a photographic negative. Am I beginning to see the world through Alice's eyes? Above the white hills the sky is darkening to lavender. Perhaps the forecast was correct. Just suppose we were snowed in. Incommunicado for weeks on end. How good would that be?

I drive the thought out, along with the residue of angst. Time enough to consider all that business later. Alice is sure to have something to say, now she's had time to process the basics. That may be what the pre-dawn walk was all about.

The door of the converted cowshed judders open. My last time here, eighteen months back, she'd just had it done. It seemed brighter then. Bigger. Clutter has shrunk it, also the cobwebs across the box window. So too, in a peculiar way, the waft of turps and linseed. Because Alice is one for the old ways. Told me she even stretches her own canvases; would grind her own colours if she could get the ingredients.

The sink area, where I set down the pot, is the most cluttered of all. Towels and rags, rainbow-streaked, dried into elaborate forms; jars of brushes like porcupines; rolled-up tubes, half-squeezed; little turds of colour everywhere. The old CD player is paint-daubed. About the floor are leaves of yellowed paper, charcoal-smutted. Also, an enormous quantity of flotsam she's dragged in from the surrounding fields. Contorted branches; stones like prehistoric eggs; sundry bits of bark. There's a bird's skull, finely sutured; the yellow jawbone of a sheep. There's a twist of barbed wire with tufts of wool like bog cotton; an encyclopaedic variety of feathers. Also of bottles.

Would be an Aladdin's cave for Jen. Impossible, now the car is ... Not that Leonora would ever have allowed it.

I have a sneezing fit. The dust has got to me. I all but overturn an easel angled toward the light. On a canvas smudged with ochre and sienna she's worked out the form of a wind-tormented tree. A blackthorn, at a guess. Must get bleak hereabouts, all the same. I'll take the city, for all its traps. Besides the work in progress there are perhaps two dozen canvases stacked about the walls. Something unspoken, some piety, holds me from having a nose through them while Alice is up the village.

Clang and groan at the gate. The crunch of tyres, then the slow growl of a car edging down the driveway. Not Alice's, though. Not a 4x4. Pressing myself to the dust-smeared window I can just see the tip of a white bonnet. A Ford? I move tentatively through the debris of the studio and, tentatively, pull the door shut. Then I edge back to the window. Footsteps, heavy, male. 'Hallo!' Rap of a fist at a door, then the lighter tap at a window. 'Anybody home?' Then I hear someone swinging heavily into the car, and the car door slam.

But the bonnet doesn't move off. I've a hunch, heavy as cement inside my gut. To give it certainty I edge back over to the door, my hand resting on the latch. I want to catch sight of that car as it drives off. It has just reached the gate by the time I make the courtyard. Red and yellow diagonal stripes, luminous. I could have scripted them. Dublin reg. But I've missed catching a decent sight of the driver.

When Alice returns I decide not to confront her with it; not at once. See if she gives anything away in her movements. In her expression or lack of. Fred is as strange with me as when I'd first arrived. 'What's the matter trooper, huh?' Bad experience of people no doubt before Alice came along with her unassailable independence. I help carry in the groceries, ignore the newspaper stuck conspicuously on top. A first brief flurry of snow, like a forethought, then the air is clear again.

Alice is packing the fridge, her back to me. 'Who was out here, Gerry?'

'When?'

Still with her back to me she straightens. 'They left the gate open.'

'Oh yeah?' Her shoulders seem aware that I'm watching them. 'I was out for a stroll.' No comment. I try a gobbet of truth. 'Oh, the phone rang. Went on for an age.' Now she's pinching dead leaves from a pot plant between thumbnail and finger. She still hasn't turned around. 'You don't have it set up for voicemail?'

'Never got round to it.'

'I'll do it. Take me two minutes.'

Now she turns. 'Don't bother. I prefer not to know.' Her face is imperturbable. If she'd anything to do with that little Garda visit, she's giving nothing away. Instead, she's looking at me with quizzical irony. The older sister.

'I dropped that saucepan down to your studio, Al. Barely got in the door.' The disarray, so unlike their married household. 'I'm surprised you can find anything in that junk shop.'

'Think I might spend a couple of hours *in that junk shop* after lunch. You don't mind?'

'Why would I mind?'

The paper is lying folded on the counter, plain as a question mark. I lift it, baton-like, tap it against my palm. 'Think it'll snow? Any chance we might get *marooned* out here?'

She shrugs. 'It's too cold for snow.'

'I never know what that means.'

Fred is looking at her intently, as though she knows.

After lunch, when I've the house to myself, I flick through the paper. There's nothing at first glance. But then, the story would be three days old by now. On the second pass I find the article, tucked in under a photo of Ryan Tubridy. A single paragraph, nothing new or solid. I leave it lying for Alice to find. Time to come clean. All I'd said, I'd left the scene of an accident. Smacked into a parked Merc at the entrance to the housing estate, must've done some damage to judge by the state of my own car. I'd panicked. Over the second bottle I'd told her I'd let my road tax lapse.

Through the window, an iodine sky. She's left the door of the studio open, and an oblong of butter-coloured light stretches across the cobbles like an invitation. Up here in the dim interior the house has begun to tick. The fridge hums, intermittently. You can actually hear the clock's slow advance. And perhaps that's good, because I need to think. So ok, I'd told her I'd panicked. It was no lie, I had. What I'd neglected to mention was *why* I'd panicked, and what might happen next on account of it. I did point out, if Prize Bitch got wind of an accident, any accident, I could kiss access to my daughter goodbye. Little Jen.

That wasn't the half of it, of course. But the rest isn't for now, either. Time enough, during the next bout of insomnia. For now, there's plenty to be getting on with. Number one, had that been Donal Walsh earlier on? After all, a D reg was hardly conclusive. Half the Garda cars in Wicklow were likely as not D reg. Number two, if it had been, was it my sister tipped him off? Made sure not to be here when we had our little tête-à-tête. But it was hard to reconcile that kind of trick with the Alice I was coming to know. Besides, when would she have done it? Not from the landline or I'd surely have heard.

But then, if it hadn't been Donal Walsh what did that mean? That they were looking out for a banged-up Yaris?

I'm revived by a blast of cold air. Alice enters, dragging with her a swirl of white dust. Face red, the half-moon scar in her temple glossy as mica. The dog is behind her, fur puffed out and dandruffed. Against the window, flakes blurred to the size of feathers are descending. *Brrrrrrr!* she goes.

'So much for your *too cold for snow ...*' I move to the window, drag my palm across the condensation. 'Any chance it'll stick?'

'Hard to say. Probably.' She's beside me, filling the kettle from a stuttering tap. But she doesn't look at me. The years have given the pale skin beneath the eyes something lizard-like; her description.

'Alice, you been in touch with Donal at all?'

'With Donny? When?'

'That car earlier,' I go on, too late now to stop, though I'm damned if I know what made me start. 'That was the guards.'

It takes a moment for her to process this. 'And you think I rang Donal?'

'Just wanted to be sure.'

Silent fury.

'Hey Al, I'm not even certain it *was* him.'

She's slapped down the kettle. 'Fuck you, Gerry! You know? Fuck! You!'

Fewer stars out, tonight. Wind more sound than motion, though high up stratospheric winds are shredding the indigo. A lunar light is shining up from the earth. It doesn't feel quite as cold as last night despite the fields of snow. Christ I hope it really does come down tomorrow. Fill up the valley with white forgetfulness. I tip the dregs into my glass, shut my eyes. 'A man is driving a cab,' I begin. Because all afternoon, the newspaper has lain where I'd left it, unread. 'Eyelids like lead. He's pretty damned tired. Been waiting on fares nine, ten hours ...'

'Had you been drinking?'

'Just listen, Alice. The guy is half-asleep, sponge-headed you know? Moonlighting all hours to try to keep up with the payments to his ex. Kid in preschool. Can't take a chance on losing access. Does nixers. Fares off the clock. Next thing the insurance premium shoots up fifty percent. Just like that! No reason.'

'Gerry, you need to ...'

'Listen. Please.' I breathe in roughly. 'Ok I should've, I dunno ... taken a *loan* out. It was stupid not to renew. But I was so fucking angry. When you're at wits' end you're stupid. Look. Alice.' Now or never. 'It wasn't a parked car I hit.' I wait. Nothing. I look toward her. In the moonlight she is as still as alabaster, the dog beneath her an effigy of loyalty. 'Back road, out behind the airport. I'd dropped off a fare. Lights turn amber. I'm pulling onto the Swords Road, punching an address into the GPS and the next thing there's this awful thump. A face ghost-white like it's caught in a flashbulb. A slump of something heavy thrown against the windshield. The car rocks, everything over in a second. By the time I've reacted they're a hundred yards behind me. One of them is staring after.'

'Who ...?'

'Girls on a night out. I've no tax, no insurance. I ... I keep driving.'

'What are you saying to me?'

'Just listen. Ok?' I pull from beneath me the newspaper. It's difficult to read the fickle print. But I could almost recite it, and I tap it as if she too has read it. *'No change in the victim's condition.* So she's no worse anyhow. *Her friend stated the taxi had its lights off.* Not true. *A coupé, possibly silver,* which *is* true; but half the Dublin taxi fleet must be coupés, possibly silver. Blah, blah. The guards following a definite line of enquiry. A fresh appeal, *for anyone who might have been in the vicinity ...'* Heart thumping, I hold out the paper toward her but she shakes her head. 'No mention of CCTV or Hailo or ... But then, that might be their definite line of enquiry, yeah? Something they're holding off releasing, you know.'

'Jesus, Gerry. Did you say she's in intensive care?'

I squint at the print, letting on. 'It says Tallaght Hospital.'

'Here. Show.'

'Intensive care, yep.'

'Jesus, Gerry.'

'Now you see why I can't call Donal Walsh?' I'm letting it out, finally. The exquisite fuck-up I've landed myself in. 'This comes out, goodbye licence. And goodbye licence, goodbye Jen. You of all people should realise what that means, Al.' Translucent shapes are drifting inside my eyelids, zooplankton seen on a slide. 'Sorry, that was a lousy thing to have said.'

The hammer of my pulse is hurting my throat. I try to guffaw. 'Told the fella up in Blessington I'd hit a sheep. Even tucked tufts of wool from a fence into the bumper. I'd all night to think up that one.'

A minute goes by, or the guts of. The moon is a sly grin. The night, listening. 'So now you have it, Al, the whole beautiful picture.' Silence, except for a low static, nature recalibrating. 'You still think we can bring in Donal?'

'Gerry, you have to tell them. You have to come clean.'

A surge of panic. 'Have you heard a word I've said?' I slap the paper. 'It says the girl's ok ...'

'Something like this. You can't not tell them.'

'Yeah but it says she's alright. The girl is alright ...'

'You told me yourself a police car came out.'

I'm standing. Guilt, not panic, has made a fist in my throat. It hurts to speak. 'The girl is going to be alright, Al.'

Night drive. At every turn the headlights spring ghost branches out of the hedgerows. Fine upward flurries, lit to sparks. The surface scintillates like granite; tire tracks to either side are dark and shallow and singular. We're scarcely making twenty miles an hour. 'The road doesn't seem all that bad!' It's the fourth time I've said it. I'm jittery as all hell.

Alice keeps her eyes to the windscreen. 'We won't be any use to anyone if we wind up in the ditch, mister.' But of course what I'm hoping, she'll say it can wait till morning. But she doesn't trust me. No more than I trust myself. *Gerry, you have to come clean.* If we wait till morning I'll have reasoned myself out of it.

From the radio the low strains of a spooky Billie Holiday track. It brings us up to the news bulletin. I await the signature, heart hammering. Gut hollowed by dread. As the song ends Alice edges up the volume. There is an interminable delay; a bad connection, out here in the pristine night. Then an aspirate crackle, as if a breath is being drawn in. Then the newscaster. Her very first report, Tallaght Hospital.

Alice pulls into a lay-by. She turns off the radio.

The hazards are dyeing the night with intermittent orange. Every noise is amplified, the tick-tick, the groans of our jackets. I want to say, now we have to turn back. I want to say, now it's jail time we're talking.

Intermittent, the hazards go on ticking, ticking.

BOUILLABAISSE

The doorbell jangled at thirteen minutes to seven. 'Christ,' she sighed. 'Don't let it be Harry.'

She wiped her fingers in the apron, cast a reproving eye at the cooker, cast an approving eye about the living room, consulted the mirror, pushed a stray lock behind an ear, click-clacked down the hallway, watched Harry's head distend and distort like a ball of India rubber through the frosted glass. *Why* could he not realise when you said seven you meant half-past at the *earliest*?

Serena took a moment, manufactured a smile. 'Harry!' Anorak dandruffed with snow. Hair combed across the dome of his scalp. The pinched red nose. The lopsided smirk as from behind his back he bungled a bunch of blue.

'Oh how lovely!' Where to stick them? 'I'll ...' she gestured intransitively.

He snuffled. 'Am I a tad early?'

She guffawed. Harry Baggot was making a slow show of wiping his feet. The first time he'd been to her flat he'd trailed half a dog turd through the lambswool carpet, and this wry display had become something of a ritual.

'Doesn't matter how much I try not to be,' he orchestrated his eyebrows into twin inverted commas as though framing an epigram, 'I always seem to be the first to arrive!' 'Well,' she began. But an aspirated, furious rattle from the direction of the kitchenette made her drop the search for a platitude and all but drop the hyacinths. 'Make yourself at home!' she remembered to call over her shoulder.

It was the bouillabaisse that was foaming over, a tide of ale-coloured froth already festering on the rims of all four rings. She stared exasperated at the fat green stems splaying in her hand. Where to ...? Sink! But a blancmange cowered in the sink. Suddenly all the surfaces were cluttered. So she backed into the living room, winced apologetically to where Harry Baggot, still in his anorak, had occupied the sofa and was readying the launch of one of those unfunny anecdotes he'd, of course, have prepared in advance − he'd have exhausted the repertoire long before anyone arrived, and for the rest of the soirée would smile inanely or violate inanely the order of books and dvds − she took in in an instant how perilously close he was to the arrays of canapés, had no time to articulate a prohibition, dropped the stems ineptly across the armchair, cascaded back through the bead strings into the galley kitchen.

Riding the spitting surf were prawns' antennae and fragments of mussel shell. No time to pussy foot. Between tea-towelled forearms she lifted the heavy pot. She almost dropped it as the ballast shifted. At once she was faced with the same problem. Every surface was occupied. If she'd just had the time to set out the delft, before the doorbell ... But, of course ... or if she could just trust that eejit to remove one *solitary* tower of plates out onto the living room table?

She heard him bark a voluminous sneeze. Had he perpetually that head cold? And, of course, never a hanky in sight.

Her eye lit upon the pedal bin. Would it take the weight? A sputter from the cooker prompted that it'd bloody well have to. She hunkered, and was manoeuvring the copper bottom across the spring-loaded lid when 'anything I can do to he-*elp*?' yoo-hooed in through the beads.

'Not a thi-*ing*!' she sing-sang, removing her arms the barest millimetre to gauge if the support would hold. It didn't budge, but didn't convince.

Her eyes surveyed the lack of options. Within the tiny galley every surface was full to teetering. 'Hi Serena, did Trev tell you ...' began the voice from the other room. Something muffled the sentence, putting it on hold. A canapé, she'd swear it! And after the devastation he'd wrought last time! Could he not ... 'You heard, of course, about poor ole Lacey up in Accounts ...'

The floor! Like a giant crustacean she clamped the seething pot between her forearms and made to set it by the fridge, but just then her mobile, which was on the microwave, decided to bicker. The keel of the pot bumped the linoleum, the bouillabaisse swilled, a scald shocked her left arm which winced away and, skidding over a crescent of brown flotsam, the lid clattered into a corner. 'Shit! Shit!' she hissed.

'Say something?' She froze, as though hiding. The phone continued its wrangle. One eye to the beads, she lifted it, saw the name, whispered 'yeah?'

'Ree-*na*, dar-*ling*. Tre-*vor*.' A pause. A long sigh. 'Look I'm sooo sorry, hun. This is such ridiculously short notice. Unfortunately, *blah blah blah blah* ...' She held it at arm's length, a creature that had just bitten. The voice continued to witter on. She set it back live atop the microwave. Trish and Dave had already had to cancel. Couldn't find a replacement babysitter. That left just the Crowleys from upstairs, a dull couple, though *she'd* talk for Ireland. And Romana, if she could make it across the city.

The scald on her arm smarted. Through the bead strings a wheezy laugh. Evidently an anecdote had climaxed. 'Right!' she called. 'That's *too* funny!' Another outrageous sneeze. Christ sake, would he be at that lark all night?

From its squat on the floor the bouillabaisse sulked. She'd have to lift it before it scummed over. With the tail end of the towel she smeared the brown dribbles about the stainless cylinder, located and replaced the lid, hoisted it back onto the ring. *Reena?* squeaked the phone. *Hello? Hello?* The screen gave up, went dark. Behind her the beads shucked apart. 'You're sure I can't help?'

'No. really. Please.' She bundled him out. 'Make yourself entirely ... honest, I'm just ...' The irony, of course, being she'd only invited him on account of Trevor Dunne, that, and to have four and four. Inadvertently, incompetently, it was Harry who'd introduced them. A work do. And now he'd cancelled, just like that! When the whole point of the evening ...

19:10. Ok. 'Tell you what,' she called, brightly. 'Open the wine. Would you do that for me?'

Everything in the kitchenette was mocking or malicious. The blancmange wobbled *don't look at me pal*. On the draining board the eight Cheshire grins of the melon she'd begun to partition. The cooker was tight as a drum battery, rattling, bubbling, snaring. Sensing it was being watched, the ring under the rice pot rasped once, twice. She grabbed it up, *Christ!* And her elbow must have nudged a champagne flute, because it reeled drunkenly, bowed, and took a plunge into the sink, shivering with the jangle of wind chimes being slapped. 'Whoops!' called Harry, hilariously. 'Don't wash that one!'

The rice pot, where? On top of the ...?

Smell of burn. The filo!

She made to put the pot in the sink. No go. Pedal bin. *Fast.*

It threatened to slide off. Her hand vacillated by the handle. Through the bead curtain, the drone of another anecdote paused. 'Yeah?' she called. Reassured, the drone resumed. The pot was still. She turned and tugged open the oven door, pulled out an acrid billow of smoke. An electric shriek protested. Her tea towel walloped the air under the smoke alarm. 'WHICK!' it hacked, just once more. For the moment it was pacified. 'Something smells good!' sang Harry, nasally.

Eyes asquint, head averted, she sidled out the tray. The pastry wings were singed. Could they be saved? Possibly. But where to ...? A volcanic burble erupted through the bouillabaisse. She'd forgotten to turn down the bloody knob! She needed her hands. Could she balance the pastry tray across her knee? Diagonally across the sink? She turned, and turning, stepped on the toes of the pedal bin.

The lid tried to laugh open. The rice pot slid. She raised a leg to hold it. Insolently it teetered, pivoting by tiny degrees until it was ready to tip over, did so, bounced once, and disgorged its load, like semolina, across the linoleum. The lid clamped shut. It was a surface, temporarily, where she could set down her tray of singed fledglings. She'd no sooner done so than the bouillabaisse seethed over for the second time. 'WHICK!' warned the smoke alarm. 'Ah-RAFF!' sneezed Harry. 'Fuck it!' Serena cried and, not finding an alternative, she swung the great pot back onto the floor inside the brown-flecked crescent beside the fridge just as the phone pinked.

Edel Crowley. Big surprise, they were 'running late'.

'Everything ok in there?' chimed Harry.

'Ha ha ha!' she telegraphed.

Ok. All *right*. Another survey. The blancmange could be saved – only one triangular shard lay upon its nudity, so far as she could see. The rice could be scooped back in, provided *he* didn't see her do it. So she thrust a smile through the beads.

The smile froze. Harry Baggot, the anorak clumsy as a sleeping bag beside him, canapé in hand, had wrought havoc on the lovely symmetry of all three plates she'd so painstakingly prepared. It was precisely how he'd desecrated the array of *hors d'oeuvre* the previous soirée before a single guest had arrived.

'Put. That. *Down!*'

His face would have been comical if she hadn't been so close to strangling him at that moment. She marched across to the *vol-au-vent* suspended before the astonished mouth and took it from him. 'Why don't you,' she began, and her other hand found in a bowl of cashews the remainder of the sentence 'try one of these?' She looked about. 'Or a crisp, maybe?'

She turned to go. She'd walked as far as the bead curtains. But something held her from pushing through. Something she'd glanced. She turned back. There, on the coffee table ... Was that her bottle of *Nuit St George*? The guilty corkscrew squirmed beside it. The only gift she still had from ... How in the hell ...? *Where* had ...?

She looked to the dining table. The two bottles of *cab sauv* were untouched, standing sentry to the eight immaculate wineglasses. She blinked. Beside Harry, her Waterford glass tumbler, all but filled with sinful burgundy. 'Ah-RAFF!'' he roared, into his hands.

Her mouth began working silent words. But instead of voicing them, she submerged beneath the beads. For a few moments, as the cutlery drawer was ransacked, they shivered and shucked.

'Harry,' she called. 'Come in here, would you?'

19:40. Still no sign of the Crowleys. And Romana was stuck on a DART somewhere northside.

Serena walked over to the mirror, tidied the mutinous lock behind her ear. She surveyed the reflected room, turned back into the real room. She adjusted the volume of the music, prodded the repaired symmetry of the three plates of *hors d'oeuvre*, pink and beige and green. His anorak she'd stuffed into the pedal bin.

She examined her surprisingly steady fingers, the left hand, the right hand. She interrogated the bead curtains, made sure nothing was emanating from beneath them. She then picked up the tumbler of *Nuit St George* that Harry Baggot had poured. She tipped it into a wineglass, and strolled as far as the armchair. Well, he wouldn't be doing *that* again, would he?

At last, the tubular doorbell bonged its jolly two tone. The Crowleys.

'Come in! Come in!' she called, knowing full well the front door was closed.

Then she toasted the galley kitchen and deflated into the armchair, demolishing as she did so the misaligned spray of hyacinths.

STILL WATERS

After the estate flooded for the third time, Clodagh determined never to return. The thought of the dank interior, silted and filthy, filled her with reptilian loathing. She left Becky in care of her sister; was seen moving like a sleepwalker along Bridge Street. Before striking out in the direction of the weir, she placed the front door key in an envelope with only the address scribbled on it and pushed it through the bank's quick deposit shoot.

The speed of the first flood had been chilling. In the space of a night hour the water had swollen from runnels leap-frogging the tarmac to a waist deep inundation upon which boxes, toys and furniture bobbed and bumped. In the pale halo of a hand torch, a fridge (was it?) rolled its flippant back. So sudden had the upsurge been, so overwhelming, that neighbours half-dressed waded in and out of unlit houses, laughing, scarcely knowing what to save and what to abandon. She'd shivered on the high ground in pyjamas and dressing gown, soothing the baby, watching the efforts of Kyle and the others with a detachment that was, almost, amused.

For weeks not a single resident of the estate had been able to return. Long after the waters receded, walls stripped of tide-marked wallpaper exhaled a river breath whose alluvial taint blow heaters failed to dry entirely. Once the insurance assessors had ticked their peremptory clipboards, carpet and underlay, lino and flooring had been pulled up and dumped over the limbs of chairs and prostrate tables in great communal mounds to the head of every terrace. Only the electricals had been taken away for specialist disposal.

At least it had been a shared catastrophe. In the hostels where those without options were variously lodged, a grim camaraderie prevailed. Besides, the inundation had been countrywide; an event which the forecasters declared a once-in-a-century occurrence. If compensation was slow in coming, and not remotely commensurate with actual costs, the cheques went some way toward restoring morale. Neighbours began to talk up that night as a disaster movie they'd all survived, a shipwreck in a midlands town. There was much talk of a communal lawsuit which, as months went by, failed to materialise. Late November, on the anniversary, Clodagh's terrace held a party out on the common that was enlivened by fireworks.

In spite of the freak weather event the forecasters had described, the new premiums had either shot up exorbitantly or else contained a clause that excluded compensation in the case of flooding. This was the occasion of the first real dispute between Clodagh and Kyle. For an American, Kyle was cautious. Arguably, it was his careful temperament that had landed them on the new estate in the first place. She'd wanted the semi-D out on the Dublin Road that would, admittedly, have stretched their monthly repayments above the fifteen hundred they'd fixed upon. That said, the sixty thousand down was her money, a legacy from her mother. The property would be in her name. She should have gone with her instinct. But Kyle could do no wrong in those days. Besides, she'd been pregnant, and who knew what unexpected costs a baby might entail.

His caution notwithstanding, it was she who now argued for the extra cover. Kyle, with trademark smirk, attempted to play down the mathematical chances of another inundation with an argument an infant could see through. She knew damn well you couldn't *times it by a hundred, Clo, just do the math. We could buy a couple more houses for that kinda dough.* At the same time, a fivefold hike in the premium payment was outrageous. It would be difficult to meet, particularly now her maternity leave was unpaid. Rebecca was a strange, interior child – later, she'd be diagnosed as 'on the spectrum' – and needed a care Clodagh was loath to entrust to strangers.

Her stubbornness on the point surprised Kyle. She'd always deferred when it came to matters financial. 'Honey, I know you're upset, but come on ...'

'Tell you what we'll do,' she said, brightly. 'We'll ask Dee.'

'Dee? What the hell's Dee got to do with any of this?'

At least Dee works up in the Financial Centre, she thought. She didn't say it. Nor did she bring up the semi-D on the Dublin Road. She waited until he'd set off for work, then Skyped her sister.

After the call she felt deflated, even humiliated. Deirdre agreed with a roll of her eyes that of course you couldn't *times it by a hundred, just do the math.* She'd never thought quite so highly of Kyle Bradley. That said, what it came down to was Becky. To meet the sort of excess Clodagh was talking about, she'd have to go back to teaching fulltime. Bar everything else, that fivefold hike (*fivefold?* Jesus!) was out of their reach any time soon with so much refurbishment still to be broached. Face it, darling, he's got a point ...

'Ok,' she said to Becky, once the computer screen went black. 'But I can't say I'm happy about it.'

Four years went by before the second weather event. In the interim, Clodagh discovered a talent for economising. It became a fixation. It was born of necessity; the school where she'd taught, though most understanding, could no longer hold the position open for her. When Kyle was away she thought nothing of illegally strapping Becky into the baby seat beside her, collapsing the rear seats and driving ten or even twenty miles to a house clearance or a car boot sale. She became adept at surfing the secondhand websites and second-guessing which were scams. She ended up sourcing bargains for half the terrace.

She began to smoke, something she hadn't done since college days. She put together a glasshouse and toolshed. And in face of Kyle's hoisted eyebrow she developed a real knack for DIY, and even earned the respect of the floorhands in Woodie's. With business taking Kyle increasingly back to the States, she had something of a freehand about the house.

There was no lack of warning this time round. If the first flood had stolen in like a thief in the night, the second arrived with the inevitability of an advancing army. All summer – it was the wettest on record – a swollen sky had loured over the entire country, dumping its excess onto an earth already saturated. For days as she'd walk Becky through the fine drizzle along the river, Clodagh had watched with tightening gut the bloat current squirm between the banks like a restive anaconda. Toward the town, teams of men in hard hats, the fire brigade, and even a truckload of bawdy soldiers had begun to bolster the flood defences with sack upon sack of wet sand, while a pair of yellow diggers like monstrous toys rattled to dredge the riverbed. High time, because with each bulletin, the contour maps tracked the gradual approach of a double depression across the Atlantic.

On the Thursday she called Kyle. He was in Portland, Oregon, in all likelihood unaware of the impending disaster. As it happened he wasn't unaware. He'd been keeping abreast of developments on the net. 'Honey, you know what time it is?'

'Yeah. Listen I need you back here.'

'Huh?'

'It's happening again, Kyle. It's going to happen again.' Silence. Static. 'I can't cope alone.'

'What about Dee? Hun, move in with Deirdre till the worst is over. Will you do that for me?'

'Kyle. We need you back here.'

A long silence. 'No can do.' She waited. 'I *told* you this, baby, I explained I ...' But what it was he'd told her he didn't get to repeat, or if he did, it was into a deaf cell phone.

She spent Friday emptying cupboards and presses, hauling what could be moved up the stairs to Becky's room, or her own, or the bathroom. She hauled boxes filled with linen and books, CDs and pictures. She hauled up lamps, the TV and the music system. She rescued the dinner set, the espresso machine, the kettle and microwave. The fridge she emptied into a Tupperware drawer which she laid in the bath alongside the perishables and foodstuffs. A number of times she sat inert for so long that Becky tugged at her. It wasn't from exhaustion, precisely. Her eye would fix unseeing on the washing machine or the cooker, on the glasshouse or toolshed, on the sofa or the fireplace or the parquet floor, her mind vacant. Dee, who'd driven all the way from Dublin straight from work, collected Becky and a bag of her things; Clodagh scarcely roused herself to thank her.

That evening, and through the night, the terrace mounted its own vigilante action. Civil Defence had deposited several van loads of sandbags and booms which they worked to plug up each gate and doorway to the height of a child. On their macs and umbrellas, the persistence of rain was pure sound. Only within the wasp's nest about each streetlight were the orange darts momentarily galvanised. It was hard to comprehend how they presaged a deluge.

There was markedly less humour this time round. Laughter was nervous and mirthless; cordiality strained by those pulling less than their weight, those occupied with their own properties to the exclusion of all else. The river was due to peak in the early afternoon. If the riverbanks could contain it, or if the overspill was limited, the glutted beast might just pass the estate without soiling it.

By eleven they'd done all that might reasonably be done. Nothing remained but to wait and watch and hope. Maggie Ryan, who was eighty one, brought out a tray of coffee mugs and another with sandwiches. They ate them in silence. By noon, the waters began to accumulate about the storm drains and the verges. Slowly, a reflective sheen spread over the roads and the common. Word was that somewhere near the boat club a wall had subsided. Once the water began to climb their rampart of sandbags, they handed out an arsenal of spades and yard brushes, of buckets and containers with which to bale. There sounded the indefatigable chug of a water pump on loan from a building site that coughed gouts of yellow seepage back into the flood.

The level continued to inch up. Outside the dyke, a vast drab tide was drifting endlessly south.

Still they hoped.

When the blow fell, it sickened like a betrayal. A literal stab in the back. Maggie Ryan, whose house was on the lowest ground, stumbled from her doorway, deploring what was just then sobbing up over her toilet bowl. They ran to look, and saw that the floor was awash. One after another, the houses succumbed. Liquid, oily and foul-smelling, surged up through the drains and outlets with a hydraulic logic they could no longer counter. It was neither as deep nor as precarious as the first flood, but even as the bulwark of sandbags held and the main danger passed, the entire terrace was infiltrated with an ankle-deep, rust-coloured slick infected with sewage. Even the men broke down.

It took several months before Clodagh consented to move back. Kyle had installed himself in an upstairs bedroom, throwing himself vociferously into a new lawsuit to nail *that son-of-a-bitch that built the estate on a goddamn floodplain, for Christ-sakes.* She knew as well as he that this crusade was to compensate for the fall off in work now that his company was downsizing; for his lack of foresight in refusing flood cover; for his unforgiveable absence in the face of the enemy. Having lived there ten weeks he'd cleared out the ground floor and had it decontaminated, but little else. It remained cold, and musty, and entirely bare.

'Where's Becky?' he'd asked. 'She's not with you?'

'I'm leaving her with Dee,' she said. And that was that. Until such time as the place could be called a home that's where their child would remain. Looking at their bedroom, strewn with mounds of papers, with a jumble of his laundry behind the door and even several plates and pizza boxes, she added 'I'm moving into Becky's room.'

Having Kyle about the place made Clodagh realise how much she'd appreciated his absences over the previous few years. At first she felt constrained, as though she were constantly being watched. Soon, though, in their uneasy truce, it was tacitly understood that the restoration of the ground floor was her domain; his business was to shore up the support of the estate in the pursuit of communal legal redress. To be fair to him, he was tireless in this. When, as early as the second evening, she'd mentioned over a glass of wine 'you do know the developer filed for bankruptcy two years ago' he'd sat back for a minute, shuffled a few thoughts, and declared *then we'll go after the councillors, and that cowboy architect, and the whatchacallem civil engineers and whatever other sons-of-bitches signed off on this disaster zone in the first place.*

She painted. She papered. She scraped. She sought out bargains, but with little of the zeal that had marked her first mission. There was an oppressive weariness about the entire estate it was difficult to escape. A number of *For Sale* signs mouldered over the course of that year. Maggie Ryan's house was boarded up, and word was she'd moved into a retirement home. With Becky in Dublin and Kyle on half salary, Clodagh began to look for part-time work. It was fortunate that substitute teaching, when she could find it, paid reasonably well. They'd fallen several months into arrears, but no more than anyone else on the estate. She saw Becky every weekend, but rarely during the week. She even consented to Dee enrolling her in a school for children with special needs in Cabra.

One day, looking over her work – the house was passably inhabitable, but to her eye a show house, no more – she tapped at the door of their former bedroom. 'I think we should sell,' she told him.

'Sell? *How?*'

'This is no life, Kyle.' The lack of fight in her own voice surprised her. 'It's not even a home anymore.'

He stood. He removed the glasses he'd begun to wear and paced as far as the window. With his back to her and his hands in his pockets he examined the view, then slowly shook his head.

'So what are you saying? We wait around for the next big rain, is that it?'

He sighed. Again he shook his head. 'There's three, no, four *For Sale* signs on this street alone, or hadn't you noticed?'

'So what do you propose?'

'What I propose ...' he turned. In the look he fired her, something akin to animosity flared. His glasses back on he began to shuffle through a stack of papers. 'Ok, so what? We sell up? That your big idea?' Unable to locate the bank statements he required, he slapped the bundle. 'Clodagh.' Deep breath. 'So this place sells for what? Hundred fifty, hundred sixty tops. That's saying we can find some chump dumb enough to take it on, which is by no means certain. Know what that means?'

'No, Kyle. What does that mean?'

'That means, my love, we walk outta here not just with Jack shit, not just with no roof over our heads, but with a legacy debt of a hundred, a hundred ten grand. See what I'm saying? Take ten years just to clear that sort of figure. I mean, do the math. We're stuck with this, baby.'

A shiver racked her. *That's twice already you fucked up*, she thought, *you do the math*. She looked long at the man, unable even to bring him into focus.

As though it were the third term in a diminishing geometric progression, the next event arrived after an interval of two years. Once again there was plenty of warning from the Met Office. Hard-hatted men in luminous jackets arrived with their trucks and diggers and sandbags. Clodagh didn't wait around to watch. She took the bus to Dublin, turned down the offer of the camp bed in the spare room where Becky had been sleeping, and installed herself on Dee's sofa. Kyle could stay on and play at sandcastles for all that she cared anymore.

Three days later, on foot of the inevitable news reports, Clodagh removed the house key from the keyring and laid it flat on the breakfast table. 'Borrow an envelope?'

Dee shook her head. 'You're going to go through with it?'

'Yup.'

'But what will you *do*?'

She shrugged, feeling weightless. To have finally lost is a relief when one has been perpetually losing. 'Don't worry. I know we can't stay here,' she supplied, sticking her tongue out at Becky.

'That's not what I'm asking, Clo.' Dee lifted the key as if it was an artefact from an archaeological dig. 'I mean, what about Mam's money?'

'The *deposit*? My dear, that is well and truly lost.'

'So you'll what? File for bankruptcy, is it?' To fracture the surface of Clodagh's flippancy, Dee slapped the key back onto the table. 'Have you any idea what that would *mean*?'

'You're the financial expert.' Briefly, she frowned. 'People make out.' Then, to Becky, 'we'll be fine, won't we sweetie?'

Deirdre wasn't one bit convinced by the display. Her sister was being far too facetious. 'Ok. So what about Kyle?'

'He'll be in a hotel somewhere. The place is knee deep in water.'

'But I mean ... *after*.'

'It's my house, Dee. The deeds are in my name.' Becky had come to her, burrowed her forehead into her shoulder. 'Kyle Bradley has no interest in custody, believe me.' She wondered if Becky knew; a wise child. She placed a palm on the soft hair. 'You'll stay up here with Auntie Dee. Won't you, Becks?'

At least Dee had no inkling. 'And if he phones?'

Clodagh lit a cigarette. Already she could hear the weir's incessant churn. The thrill of vertigo; of letting go.

'Tell him ...' She blew an orchid of smoke into the air, as all the disdain that had accumulated for seven years concentrated in her features. 'Tell him the goddamn word is *maths*.'

The Lie

The last of the visitors had left. I was reaching for my coat when I felt Rita's hand stay my arm. She waited for the front door to click. 'Jack,' she murmured, though the house was now quite empty. 'You were his best friend.'

A foreboding of what was to follow made me look past her to where light glimmered off the dark mahogany. If that was true it was a sobering thought. Earlier I'd stood long at the coffin, emotions as inert, as finally improbable, as the waxen features inside it. I hadn't seen Ronnie Walsh in the four years since their marriage. Although I'd been best man, we'd both known that honour was already an anachronism. We'd been close in school, less so in university.

With the guests gone shadows had begun to inhabit the living room. The furniture had taken on the disturbing quality of an orphaned shoe or glove. 'Jack, I have to know.' She'd moved to the head of the coffin, her fingers not six inches from the lurid forehead. She was looking down, her face impossible to read. 'What exactly happened on the stag? He'd never say.'

In that instant, four years were abolished. I was back in Saint-Malo, two in the morning, under the great ramparts, Ronnie sitting in the wet sand, his back pressed to the city walls, face bloodied and shirt torn open.

I shook my head. 'Nothing *happened*.'

'All I know is, when he came back he'd changed.' Her voice turned an accusatory edge. 'He was never the same Ronan I'd known, after.' She poured two careful drinks, advanced deliberately, pressed one into my hand. 'You have to tell me. Please.'

'Rita ...' I again looked toward the black carapace in which was laid out the suicide, if that's what he was. The guards 'weren't looking for anyone else in connection with the death.' Ronnie'd had what they term 'history'. But what autopsy can disclose a state of mind?

I took the gin and tonic in one go, but held it long in the mouth before swallowing. I then slapped the glass on the piano, wanting to be the hell out of there. 'There's nothing to tell.'

She placed her drink, untouched, beside the empty glass. The manoeuvre allowed her to block my path to the door. 'Was he *with* someone, is that it?' I didn't answer, but a sound escaped, halfway between a gasp and a guffaw. Instantly her fists struck hard at my chest. I grabbed them, astonished at the fury with which her eyes flashed. 'I *know* he was with someone! Christ!'

For the briefest of moments, it seemed the corpse might overhear us. 'Rita for god's sake ...' Then I released her wrists. The eyes, black-lined, aged and terrible, remained fixed on me. 'Ok,' I said. Though it was not ok.

That trip to Saint-Malo had nearly fallen through. As best man it had fallen to me to organise the stag. But the names on the emails Ronnie passed on were largely unknown to me, and the few I'd recognised I'd long since lost touch with. In the end there were only five of us.

There'd been a lot of drinking all afternoon, and that raucous camaraderie that springs up between strangers thrown together for an occasion. Ronnie talked up the misadventures we'd had, I reciprocated, the others too, all of us aware that it was a pretence. In the restaurant there were toasts, jokes, execrable French, and lewd songs, each more boisterous in proportion as the place emptied and the waitress's smile grew brittle. We were the last to leave.

Outside we wandered the old citadel, getting lost, stopping at this or that terrace, tossing off another round of *Jupiler* or *Ricard*, laughing, exaggerating. The night was warm, even as the last bars began to shut. Somewhere near the cathedral Fitz, who was a cousin, took me firmly by the shoulders. 'Lap dancing *à la mode!*' he demanded, '*Monsieur le best man* will have sussed out where ...'

I removed his hands in time to see Ronan's young work colleague hunch double to splash chowder over the cobbles. 'I haven't. *Desolé.*' A simple statement of fact. I tried unsuccessfully to catch Ronnie's eye, to see what his intentions were. I'd no desire beyond bed. 'Fortunately, *Monsieur,*' Fitz brayed, raising the fallen colleague, 'I've a nose for these things. *Allons-y ...*'

Somewhere near the Grand Port the group separated. I'm unsure if it was I or Ronnie who'd nudged the other and made the equivocal gesture. We ducked through an archway, crossed an empty square, came out somewhere on the far side, descended a stone ramp. I recall a damp forest of timbers sunk into the sand, a glint on the black water. He squeezed my shoulder. 'This must be a terrible bloody bore for you.'

'No, I'm ...'

'Course it is. I appreciate it. I mean *all* of it.' He turned a lopsided grin. 'You don't think much of Rita, do you?'

I broke from him. 'Kinda question is that?'

He was after me, laughing. 'Wait.' He drew level. 'Stop, would you?' I did so. But I'd no intention of letting him repeat the absurd question. 'Ronnie, I've scarcely seen you since ...'

His hands were up. 'I know. I know. My fault.'

'It's no one's fault. It's life. You know, *life*?' Then it struck me he may have misunderstood my 'since ...' to mean 'since the breakdown'. From our earliest schooldays he'd been prone to anxiety, and in the year of our finals, panic attacks led to a sojourn in John of Gods. There'd been talk of self-harm. 'Since you and Rita began seeing each other, guess we've left each other alone. It's par for the course, no?' I met and held his eye. In school he'd rarely allowed anyone besides myself to do that; a trust that impressed the teachers. 'I was *glad* when I heard you'd found someone.'

His eyes flitted from mine to an imaginary spot to my left, a trait I recognised of old. A tangential line of thought was coming. 'The Greeks had the same word for soul as for butterfly, you know that, Jack? *Psyche*.' His eyes interrogated, desperately. 'Why a *butterfly*? Why not ... a bird or something? Hunh! What d'you see when you think of a soul?'

'Jesus I don't know.'

Then his eyes were back to the left. 'See, we let our lives grow hard around us. Husks and habits, dead end jobs. Relationships that cool into crusts ...' He began staring into his palm as if some wisdom might be written there. 'I don't *love* Rita.'

'You don't?'

'Not the way she means the word.'

'Does she know you don't?'

The glance he threw in reply was something from the back of the classroom.

'Then why in god's name marry her?'

Eyes left. 'Habit is armour. I guess as we grub through life there's nothing better. Nothing we can *choose*, you know, Jack? Don't tell me you're any different! So life becomes a cocoon we crawl inside. Comical, isn't it? But just maybe, all the while, inside, the soul's pupating. Course we don't *see* any wings. We know nothing about it. *Nada*.' He was grimacing. 'Know what death is? The armour cracks open, and we fly the cocoon.'

It had grown colder. 'I don't get it. You're *looking* for a routine, is that it? Jesus, you'd want to tell her if that's all you're after. Because believe me, she ...'

'What I'm saying, *Jack*,' he all but spat my name, 'if our lives have any beauty at all, we know nothing about it. Maybe god or someone sees it.' Then his hands opened, as if letting the thought go. 'She wants kids. Hey, that's fine by me. A kid would ... solve a lot of things.'

'What d'you want me to say to you, Ron? You want my *blessing*, is that it?'

Suddenly he had me in a headlock. We began a crazy dance over the sands, the sort of rough horseplay I'd grown to expect when we were in school. That night it didn't feel like horseplay. The grip was fierce. All at once we were scrapping. I banged my head painfully off one of the stumps, hurled him against the wall. He came back at me like a rabid animal. Then, as quickly, his fury was spent. My clothes were wet and sandy, my head hurt. I was in no mood for his antics. 'Where you going?' he called.

'Hotel.'

I was halfway up the ramp when I felt him tug my arm. 'Please, Jack. I'm going crazy here. There's no one I can talk to.'

'How about Rita? God's sake, look at you!' He really did look a sorry state, jacket lost, shirt torn, eyes watery and blood scabbing under his nose.

'Ten minutes, Jacko. That's all I'm asking.'

'Ten minutes.'

We returned to sea level. His back against the damp wall, he slid down and ploughed his feet through the sand like a drunk. 'She's seven years older than me, d'you know *that*?'

'You told me.' But he hadn't. I squinted down at him. 'Is it *seven*?'

'I imagine I told you three.'

'So then she's ...?'

'Forty, December.' He was laughing again. 'I only found out yesterday. Get this. I'm looking for my passport, yeah? Rita's at work. Normally she looks after that end of things. For the life of me I can't remember if she'd said she left it out. So I'm going through where she keeps stuff and I come across *her* passport. All these years I'd never seen it. And that's when I find out. December '73.'

'But ... so she'd lied to you?' Silence. 'All these years she's lied about her age.'

'What's a lie?' His eyes were shut, now. 'She never *lied*. I mean, she knew I *thought* she was three years older. One time, I'd guessed '77 and she'd sort of gone along with it. Let on to be mad with me that I'd guessed. But she'd never actually *said* it.'

'Still, Ronnie, not to clear it up ...'

'Course the irony is, the whole bloody thing about getting married was the body clock thing, you know? At thirty six she simply wasn't going to have time to find someone else and start over.' His head was thrown back against the wall, his eyes fixed on a distant gleam on the sea: a ship, a lighthouse. 'Guess we're closer to midnight than we thought.'

'So ... you're going to tell her.'

He looked up at me, surprised to find anyone there. 'Tell her what?'

'That you found out how old she is!'

'God no.'

'And the wedding?'

'I can't ... be *alone*.'

And that was it. The entire story. Was I supposed to tell it her?

Rita had moved over to the blinds and was peering at the streetlight. Her shadow reached into the gloomy interior, though not quite as far as the effigy which, however I might try, I couldn't square with my old school friend. Looking about the vacant furniture I tried to imagine their four years together. If his death had been, as they say 'doubtful', at what point had all this become unbearable? When children were no longer feasible? Or was it the old anxiety, those butterflies that no routine could quiet?

Finally, he *was* alone.

I assumed they'd tried IVF. Rita was nothing if not methodical. But wouldn't the truth of her age have come out then? Or had she managed to conceal it, even as she'd taken charge of all the paperwork at the time of the wedding? Perhaps there'd been tears. Confessions. Who knows, a reconciliation? Perhaps he'd admitted he'd known all along. But had Ronnie ever told her his cold truth: that he didn't love her, had never loved her, in all likelihood could never love her, not in the way she intended the word?

I looked at her back, hunched against the next thirty years.

'The night of the stag,' I began, 'we brought him to this lap dancing club ...'

THE MEMORY OF THE DAY

He's not supposed to come anywhere near the school. Joey told me. He's only supposed to come visit us up in Uncle Tommy's house. And that's only on Sundays. And not even every Sunday, just some Sundays. Mam would throw a fit if she knew he was here waiting for us.

Joey started in the community school this year. But after school he's supposed to wait for me by the gate coz I'm too small to walk home on my own. The gate is where Daddy's car is parked. He's not supposed to be parked there. But when I get up to the car I can see that Joey's already sitting in the front seat, so I get in. There's a smell of burn.

'Hey, Joey,' I say.

Joey's all quiet today. So I start kicking the back of his seat. 'Quit it!' he says. Daddy's not saying anything either. He just starts driving. Usually he winks at me in the mirror, but today he doesn't. Mam told Joey he was to stop calling him Daddy coz it'd only confuse me, which is really stupid. The time we visited him in the rest home we called him Daddy. He had a breakdown and he was wearing a dressing gown and his face was all scratchy coz he didn't shave for ages. A breakdown is when you stop speaking to anyone. But that was back when we were still living up in the big house.

Daddy used to be a developer. I don't remember that time but everyone says that's what he was. A developer is when you build houses. Miss Flanagan told the class he used to be the biggest developer in all of Leitrim. That's how come we had such a big house and everything. But then it all went wrong and then Mammy took us to move in with Uncle Tommy. That was after Daddy had the breakdown.

Before Joey went to the community school he was always getting into fights with the twins from the Riverside Estate. 'Your da's not such a big shot now, is he?' That's what they were always shouting at Joey. The Riverside Estate never got finished and all the families had to be moved into a hostel coz the toilets didn't flush properly. One morning when we were supposed to be going to school someone smeared poop all over our front door. Mammy was crying and shouting at Daddy and she wouldn't let us go out that day.

Uncle Tommy's not our real uncle. He's mammy's friend. But we always called him Uncle Tommy. He used to work for Daddy but he doesn't any longer. We've been living up in his house ever since the bank took the big house back. He's all right, I guess, except for when he fights with Joey. Once, he smacked Joey twice on his behind and Mammy shouted 'don't you dare touch that child!' Joey was shouting 'you're not my dad' and then he bit him on his hand and he wouldn't let go and you could see afterwards the mark. That's when Uncle Tommy smacked him. After that he was locked in the room until he said he was sorry. But I don't think he ever said it.

We're not going up to Uncle Tommy's now so I ask 'where are we going Da?' Daddy just looks at me in the mirror. He doesn't say anything. There's black on his face, like soot or something. And there's black on his hands as well. That must be where the smell of burn is coming from. Joey's just looking out the window. I suppose we're going for a drive. But then at the sign we take the turn for the lake, so I suppose we're going to the lake. When Joey was little Daddy used to take him down to the lake all the time. He has this boat down there, and sometimes he used to allow Joey to row. I was always too small, but sometimes he used to allow Joey. He even allowed him to hold the motor with Daddy's hand on top of his hand.

The pier is all bockedy, but still you can walk on it if you're careful. That's where the boat is tied up. It's all wet and Daddy says 'jump in and bale her out, there's a great girl.' To bale is when you throw out the water with a tin of soup. There's loads of water in it coz no one's taken it out for ages and it's all rusty coloured. When I get in the boat it rocks and the water sloshes about, but then when I sit down it stops and you can hear the waves against the bottom. 'The gossipy waves,' Daddy used to call them. Mammy told Uncle Tommy he was always queer in the head.

Joey doesn't help me to bale coz he's to help Daddy carry stuff out of the boot. He needs Joey to help coz there's a basket with loads of stuff in it, and a plastic can of petrol, and the motor which is really heavy and has this propeller at the end, and Daddy's rifle case. It's green and has straps. Joey is looking at Daddy kind of funny after he gives him the rifle case. 'Why do we need the gun?' he says. 'We'll shoot a few rabbits.' 'Where?' 'On the island.' He rubs Joey's head but Joey crinkles up his forehead and speaks at the ground. 'There's no rabbits on the island,' he says. 'We'll see,' says Daddy. That's what he always says when you ask him for something, but then afterwards he always says yes. Or nearly always.

I'm not big enough to take any of the things so Joey has to get into the boat with them. It rocks when he gets in. Daddy passes the basket down to Joey, and then he passes the plastic can of petrol, and then the rifle. 'Be careful with that,' he says. 'Lie it down on the floor.' He looks all serious like when he used to get letters from the bank and everything. Then he gets in and the boat rocks all over the place. The motor is too heavy even for Joey, and he has to take it off the pier himself, and then he has to tie it on so it doesn't fall off.

I put my foot on the rifle case. It's heavier even than an oar. Daddy used to go hunting with it when we were still up in the big house. One time he took Joey with him and they shot a rabbit. There was this big scab on its head when he hung it up in the garage. Mam threw a fit when she found out he'd taken Joey with him. 'Jesus are you trying to kill the child?' That was ages ago though.

Daddy's elbow has to pull at the engine loads of times before it starts, and then there's this big blue cloud and the engine goes thug thug, but then when we start to move out into the lake it sounds more like a lawnmower and the boat tilts up. The water's brown and there's a long line of yellow bubbles behind us so you can see where we came from. We're headed for the island in the middle of the lake which has all trees on it. Joey told me they went out there a couple of times to catch eels. It's hard to see where the rabbits would go though. It's only the same size as the schoolyard. And anyway it's going to get dark soon and then you wouldn't be able to hunt rabbits. One time when it got late I asked Daddy how come the lake was full of bright. Daddy just messed my hair. 'It's bright with the memory of the day,' he said.

It doesn't take long to get to the island but then you have to be careful coz it gets all shallow and there's mud and branches and rocks and reeds. Daddy steps into the water and it comes up past his knees. There's a cloud of midges around his head and everything through it looks blurry. Midges make you itchy. But the midges are coz it's getting dark. Daddy lifts us out of the boat and onto the island, first Joey and then me. But when I ask does Mammy know we're out here he says 'your Mammy's fine, don't worry about your Mammy.' And I'm not. But Joey has a strange look like I've seen him sometimes when he thinks Uncle Tommy is telling us fibs or something.

Daddy pulls a big towel out of the basket. 'Put that around your shoulders, Katie, *a pheata*,' coz on the boat I started shivering. He sounds all hoarse, like when you have a sore throat. It's still not all that cold, but I put the towel around me and I sit on the basket and swing my legs. 'You wait here *a leana* won't you?' he says and he nods to Joey to come on. 'Where are we going?' Joey asks. Daddy doesn't say. He just puts his hand on his shoulder and then he leads him off into the woods. When Joey looks back at me he looks scared.

They're gone for ages. It's starting to get darker now. After a while a car comes beside the pier where Daddy's car is parked. It's far away but you can hear it like it's close. It's a white police car like the one Sgt O'Meara drives. She's a Ban Garda. Once she had to come into the school when someone broke all the windows of the big house. But maybe it's not her, it's too far to see. 'Daddy!' I call. There's a lump in my throat because I'm crying and my nose is runny. 'Joey!'

When they come back Daddy's face is all wet. His eyes are red like he's been crying too. He doesn't have the rifle with him. And even though it's dark I can see that Joey is all white and his eyes are big and he's shaking like when he's been in swimming and there's a wind afterwards. I run over to him and stick my head into him. 'Take Katie back over, Joey,' says Daddy and his voice is even more hoarse now. And then we all get into the boat. Then after he starts up the engine Daddy gets back out of the boat.

'Tell your mother ...' he says. But he doesn't tell Joey what he has to tell Mammy. Then he pushes us away. 'Da!' I call him. 'Are you not coming, Da?' But he's not. He just goes back into the woods without looking back at us.

All the way back to the pier Joey is shaking. He won't say anything, even when I ask him how Daddy's going to get back. He just looks past me. 'But how is Daddy supposed to get back?' and I kick his foot because I'm crying, but he still won't look at me. Over Joey's shoulder I can see the trees on the island are moving up and down. They look like cardboard coz it's dark. Then the sky over them goes black with crows. Then there's this bang. You can hear the echo roll all around the lake.

FUGITIVE

I

Oscar Finn closed one eye and contemplated the scene through the quadrilateral frame of finger and thumb, finger and thumb: constellations of motes trapped and turning slow as mobiles in the tobacco light that leaned intermittently through the slats. *Striated.* That was the term. What sort of exposure would that require?

He moved the rough rectangle laterally until it had framed the trap; the crude box propped on a stick, the rough blue twine, the trail of seed dribbled across the moonscape of humus and cowpat. *Follow twine with eye of a creature scurrying to close-up shot; a ticking acoustic.* Four, five seconds. *Cut to doorway, the frozen land beyond; score by Ennio Morricone ...*

A yawn was curtailed by a spasm, deep and animal. 'God I could get used to this,' he hugged his shoulders, 'if it wasn't for the bastard cold.' It had been two days since they'd eaten anything more substantial than crisps and chocolate bars and an occasional filched egg; two nights since they'd slept anything but an intermittent, fitful sleep. They'd seen off the dregs of the first night in a ruined industrial plant somewhere beyond Carlow, a vast, chalky interior that smelt of dust and ammonia and dead pigeons. It had been draft prone, the ground stubborn and uneven.

But at least there had been cloud cover. On the second night, though, the sky had bared its teeth. Four degrees of frost the forecast had predicted; it could as easy have been fourteen. *She* had known, some feral wisdom had told her, that banks of fodder had hot, fermenting innards, otherwise they might quite literally have frozen.

Ten to one she'd still be lying there wide awake, alert as a cat, figuring their next move under folds of matted cud that were merely dank now. 'Hoy,' she'd warned him, '*don't* come back with anything less than a chicken, you hear? I mean it Oscar Finn!' He'd been swabbing the damp remains of grass, white and rotting, from his leathers. 'And how are we supposed to cook a chicken for god's sake, you thought about that?' Silent, she hoisted an interrogative eyebrow. A vision took him, her lovely mouth tearing into a bloody-feathered breast. 'You're hardly proposing we eat the thing raw?'

'I'll figure that out. You just go get the stupid bird, ok?' Pause. 'Ok?'

'Ok ok, Jesus! But if I do manage to feck one, it'll be up to you to pluck the *stupid bird*, yeah?' A thought had halted him in his tracks, and he'd returned briefly. 'Not to mention, you can throttle the bloody yoke.' She offered him a glower, almost, before she'd rolled back over. 'Seriously, Yazzer, I wouldn't know where to begin, me!' And as he'd stepped shivering into the pre-dawn, ghost-lit from beneath by the mineral frost, a whispered afterthought took him: *Have you killed living creatures, Yasmin Hasan, in whatever incarnation it was you were living before you came over here?*

How many hours had he been absent from their bower by this time? He tried to estimate without consulting his watch. A white-haired sun had risen long since, but never quite clearing the leafless hedgerows that edged a land turned to quartz. He'd scouted the perimeters of a couple of farmhouses, trying to gauge from a distance the vigilance of their dogs. He'd made one approach to the rear of a chicken coop, scarcely more than a stack of crates held together by hexagonal wire. He'd crawled under a fence, had lain low, had watched the dead windows of the farmhouse, knelt up, slipped the catch, jerked the door ajar. Outside was a pewter dish from which he'd scooped up a handful of seed. He spilled half into his jacket pocket, laid half on his open palm. His first, ever so tenuous foray, advancing the palm into the airless, intimate interior was met by an eruption of obstreperous gargling, then a hoarse cascade of barks toward the house that sent him tumbling helter-skelter back over the fence and through tangles of frozen brambles.

Later, the frigid air scraping throat and lungs, he'd stumbled through a pane of ice up to the knee in vice-cold silt. He'd hunkered behind a nettle sieged bathtub while a grey Landover trundled slowly, slowly up a hill, and had only become aware of the nettles when they wickedly scalded his wrists. He'd been about to give up, to return empty-handed when, a bare field short of where they'd kipped the night before, he'd faltered upon the old wooden outhouse, a barn of some kind or a stable. He'd have passed in sullen silence, not bothering to look inside, but for a jerky movement in the thicket that crowded an ice-toothed water barrel: the pneumatic, preposterous clockwork of a hen.

How much time had passed since that unlikely vision? *Pan to interior, ceiling shot.* Oscar Finn the hunter gatherer lying prone. He has been propped on his elbows for so long that they are cramped, his body rigid with the cold, his eyes sore and itching, his belly indented by cakes of muck. A length of rough blue twine he'd salvaged from a fence trails as far as a contraption, the cunning of which would hardly fool a three year old. And yet now, and now, very now, into the viewfinder of his fingers, there has chanced in stop frame, the perpetually startled mechanism of the fowl.

Oscar dares not breathe. Infinitesimally, the hen advances. Infinitesimally, his finger winds the twine a turn, a second, taking up the slack until it lifts the merest flick from the earth. Through tines of striated light the scalded head burbles forwards, wobbles its wattles, clicks through discrete degrees of suspicion. It tips, pecks, clucks, struts. It side-eyes the balancing contraption that overhangs the mound of seed as if assessing the millet in the riddle. Nothing exists outside its avian calculus. 'Come on. Come on now ...' Excruciatingly, it broaches the box.

And it jerks, alarmed! A sudden shadow has fallen from the doorway ...

All at once it squawked, fluttered, stuttered into flight. Instinct tugged the string and (fuck it!) the box fell on vacancy. But even as it did, the bird balled up, hurled sideways, an animated feather duster driven tumbling across the muck-caked floor. In tandem, a half brick skipped through the muck. Dazed, its mechanism broken, the bird skirted the wall as a series of victory ululations echoed to the rafters.

'Jesus Christ, Yazzer! You put the heart across me, you did!' He levered himself stiffly up, clumsy with the static of pins and needles. He squinted at the silhouette, brushed in curt strokes the muck from his jacket. 'I had it all under control you know.'

'You had, yeah, I could tell. So go get it, Irishman!'

'Ok, I will. Only like I say, I'm not plucking the fucker, but.' He shook his head at her, made in manly steps for the corner into which the hen was now collapsed. It no longer moved, merely palpitated, its eye unblinking, one wing an extended lady's fan that might have been nailed to the planking. Oscar Finn made a number of tentative passes before her jeers had him tugging it abruptly up by the legs and thrusting it into her amused hand. Before they emerged into the blue daylight, in a single flurry of soughing wings the neck was disarticulated.

All the way back as he stumbled over granite drills a dozen steps behind, he watched the bundle slap against the rhythm of her stride. Knee-high boots, jeans faded and faintly brindled, a pinched leather jacket; a body that moved with animal ease. Feline, he would have said of her, if it wasn't for her visceral aversion to cats. *Eyes to die for*, the tagline would go, gravelled cinema trailer voice. But what did he really know about Yasmin Hasan? What did any of them know about her?

II

The fact was, Oscar Finn couldn't even be sure of the event that had precipitated their flight to the north. It began with a dramatic rat-tat-tat at the door that was more than insistent. Its stutter had erupted into the student flat, had pulled himself and Nige out of their respective slumbers. She'd stood as studied and deliberate as something from a film poster, hair a tangled storm over tight leather, shoulder straps sustaining a miniature backpack, a helmet in her hand as if she were Salome bearing the head of an infernal John the Baptist. It was Nige who'd opened the door to that magnificent apparition. 'Whose is the helmet?'

Her eyes narrowed. When he attempted nonchalance, which was embarrassingly often, Nigel Manley had the knack of winding people the wrong way. 'Come on, we're going!' she'd called over his pillow-skewed hair toward Oscar, still stumbling out of his room. 'I'll explain as we go.' Ten seconds later he was tucking a shirt tail into uncooperative leathers, was hopping into a stubborn boot, ignoring the envious irony of his flatmate's glasses flashing like twin smartphones. 'Go where?' he called to the doorway in which her absence radiated like an after image. He was so flustered he failed to notice the gloves tumble like birds from inside his helmet; if Nigel had noticed he'd said nothing about it, had yowled instead like a tom on heat.

They were already spluttering up the Dublin Mountains on his underpowered Suzuki, leaving the yellow brocade of city lights far behind, before the story began to get tossed at him in shreds and patches. 'Hunt is such an asshole!'

'Who?'

'Hunt! He's such an absolute jerk!'

Gareth Hunt, associate lecturer in film studies. Scouse. Long, greasy hair and a jowl tooled by childhood pox. Cruised around Ballyfermot on a road bike built like a sound system, 1000cc, three aerials at the least. The rumour mill had it he'd tried it on with Yasmin pretty much throughout first year. Rumour had her on the back of his bike maybe a half dozen times, not all of them patent bullshit. But then, she was the sort of girl who gave rise to rumours. Whether or not there was truth in any of them, she'd never let on either way. Hunt was fifty if he was a day and something of a barfly, even dipping his proboscis inside the SU bar. 'Would you look at the head on him,' Nige had winked to himself and Dots O'Shea during induction week. 'He's like a bleedin' try-hard Gary Moore,' which surprised more that Nigel Manley should have ever heard of Gary Moore than for any great resemblance.

That he was an absolute asshole was no epiphany. 'Why, what did he do this time?' Oscar had called back to her above the continual growl; his bike, unused to passengers, protesting the poor choice of gear. She was in no rush to answer. Perhaps she was awaiting a more level section of road. When at length they reached the N81, she leaned in, their helmets butting like pool balls. So she'd clocked him one, apparently. Hit him a clobber with the helmet (so it was his! Oscar thought he'd recognised the heraldic flames, gules, on field of sable), had left the randy fucker stretched out on the floor of his office.

'Holy shite! Yazzer, you did not ...'

'Didn't I?'

'Well ... *when*, for god's sake?'

'Couple of hours back maybe.'

He peered quickly at his watch face. 'At coming on for eleven o'clock at night? What were you doing in his office at eleven o'clock on a jaysus Tuesday night?'

That one she didn't choose to answer. And Oscar was in no state to press her on it. The man was a proven womaniser. Track record of being an asshole, with a sarcastic delivery hammered flat by his Liverpool accent, and sure of himself with the exaggerated, impregnable swagger of the underachiever. A decent enough lecturer, give him that; though why Yasmin Hasan had chosen him as dissertation supervisor was beyond reckoning. Calling her in at half ten at night would be just his style. Whether or not the powers-that-be were aware of it, it was common knowledge among the student body that he'd cut his own set of keys and kept abreast of the code to the alarm. Also, that he kept a bottle of scotch whisky in his bottom drawer, which down the years the Chinese whispers had mutated into a minibar and camp bed. So that to Oscar's way of thinking if she'd had to discourage his advances with a clatter of his helmet it was good enough for the Scouse bollocks.

Never had the world seemed so unreal. The night streamed by, cold and finely needled with drizzle. He had no idea where they were going, nor why, nor what they were supposed to do if ever they got there. He'd nothing in his wallet beyond maybe a fiver. He hadn't so much as a change of socks or boxers, let alone a spare t-shirt. She hadn't even allowed him time to lay a hand on his jaysus toothbrush. But, with Yasmin Hasan's pressure leaning into his back, he ignored the incipient frostbite on his naked fingers. He saw, in his mind's eye, a long helicopter shot, a countryside in darkness but for the single, tiny torchlight discovering the tape measure of a road.

As early as term one of their first year, Oscar had lent her his copy of Mackendrick's *On Film-Making*, a book he'd never seen since, which mightn't have been so bad if he thought for a minute she'd even once opened the damn thing. He'd shown her a handful of sites where it was possible to stream pretty much any movie for free; he'd bounced ideas with her before her tutorial presentations. Then, over the course of the previous semester, Oscar had dug her out a couple of times with her essays. She'd thrown one memorable all-nighter sprawled on their sofa, declaiming long tracts toward the ceiling that he'd translated onto her memory stick with the occasional assistance of Professor Google. Nigel had hunkered in the corner, noisily engaging his Xbox until about one in the morning, when even his talent for being a late-adolescent pain in the arse had finally wilted. Between the two of them they'd managed a 68%, not at all bad for a tract on some Palestinian director he'd never heard of, though later she was furious not to have got the first.

Alpha Nerd, she dubbed him, which if nothing else relegated Nige and Dots O'Shea to the role of sidekicks. '*Manley*, that his name? Are you *kidding* me?' she'd jibed one afternoon when she breached the vacant, poster-hung bedroom that smelled of stale maleness. Oscar chased uneasily after her, guided her back out. 'I bet you any money himself and that other chess freak you're always with speak Klingon when they're alone.'

Where Oscar was concerned, from the very first she'd made fun of his underpowered Suzuki, or else it was his improvised manner of riding it. She mocked his technologically-wired flat, and the fact he was still sharing with a geek he'd known from his schooldays, and hanging out with another he met in the chess club. She mocked his addiction to streaming classics on *Netflix*, and his ability in class to quote entire exchanges from the black and white era. But behind all that mockery, Oscar had always sensed she had a bit of a soft spot for him. Yasmin Hasan.

III

He watched her now, hunkered against a post with her eyes fixed on some distant thought, tugging feather after feather from the carcass with disconcerting ease. Was that another talent she'd picked up in the refugee camps where she'd been variously raised? Sometimes it was hard to square her precise, slangy English with such an upbringing. Her father had been a delegate of some stamp with a connection to the UN, her mother a medical worker and activist. She had an older brother who'd become radicalised and now preached Sharia law from a delinquent arrondissement of Paris, last she'd heard. She'd been in Dublin for three years. Hard to piece together the jigsaw, though, or even construct a rough chronology for it. It wasn't a childhood she cared much to talk about.

He was startled from his reverie by the bird thumping at his feet. In his life he'd never seen anything so outrageously naked; the skin livid and goose-bumped and obscenely nude but for the feather boa at its neck and ankles. The beak lay open and inanimate, the simulacrum of a beak; the eye was filmed over with a lid of mica. He rolled away from it and dry retched into the grass like a dog. 'You're not telling me,' he coughed, wiping the back of a hand across either cuticle, 'you're seriously thinking of eating that?'

'You got a better idea,' she said, no interrogation mark. She had a low smoky voice that, like an inland sea, never really rose or fell. It ill-corresponded to the volatility of her opinions. Right at that moment, anything seemed preferable to Oscar to addressing the obscenity sprawled at his feet. 'Tell you what,' he tried. 'How about we go back to that place from last night? You remember, with the barred gate and that cat you spotted?'

She shuddered, as though the animal had materialised. 'And do what, exactly?'

'Maybe, we try the door this time?'

'Brilliant. And ask them what? That's if there is an answer.'

'I don't know, Yaz. For a hot meal?'

'Sure,' she said. She moved her hands into the matted nest of her hair. 'Ask them for a hot shower while you're about it, and maybe a feather bed.'

'Well, why not?'

She didn't answer. She didn't have to. Were she to, it would be to remind him for the hundredth time. No phones. No ATMs. No toll plazas. No big towns. No talking to anyone who might recognise either one of them. For the trouble had begun, the real trouble, the morning after their first night on the road.

Toward dawn they'd forced the door on a derelict plant, had nestled for a few hours out of the wind and drizzle on a floor that would have been hard concrete but for the accretion of feathers, bird droppings and god alone knew what else. There was a spoor of ammonia that made breathing more than unpalatable. There were rattles in the rafters and scuffles along the corrugated iron that suggested pigeons or crows, but may equally have been rats. As it gradually grew bright they gave up on the place and any idea that it might afford them a few hours' kip. They continued instead another forty miles until they found a small town that was waking up, and a café that was on the point of opening. Yasmin, having apparently no cash at all on her, ordered only coffees, then they sat over the final dribbles of milky liquid for the better part of an hour. As Oscar ambled up to pay, the news came on the radio.

It was the third item. An assistant lecturer at Ballyfermot College of Further Education, unnamed, was discovered unconscious in the early hours of the morning by a cleaner; he'd suffered a fracture to the skull and a broken cheekbone; he was taken into intensive care where his condition was said to be serious but not critical; a Garda spokesman said that the nature of the injuries suggested foul play. As yet they were puzzled both as to the identity of the assailant and the possible motive for the assault, but were following a definite line of inquiry.

That was bad enough. That had sent them back onto the road with no thought of stopping until they'd hit the relative safety of the north (her idea). The only problem, they'd have to fill the tank. The gauge was long since bust, but sloshing it about suggested they'd only a couple of litres left in the tank. 'How far will that take us?' she called after a few miles.

'I don't know, to be honest with you. Hundred k?'

'You don't *know*?' At that moment, as if supplied by providence, they came upon a Topaz station, somewhere to the far side of Kilkenny. So far so good. He filled her up. What little cash Oscar had was gone but for loose change. He'd explained that to her back in the café. Now, he was blithely informed that she wouldn't chance using her Laser card. Why she hadn't mentioned that particular scruple before he'd filled the bloody tank was beyond him. His card, he'd already told her, was right at the overdraft limit. That wasn't quite true. The last tranche of rent was still available, just. He'd already fobbed Nigel off twice on that score. Stalemate. Their eyes locked. He blinked first. 'Alright! Ok! I'll give it a *lash*, Jesus!'

Reluctantly he'd queued, a couple of bags of crisps, a pack of Tampax, a Bounty bar. Behind the till the young one's thumb was weaving over her smartphone as though racing to solve a puzzle. 'Any petrol with that?' she'd asked without looking up, and before he had a chance to think it through, the lie had escaped his lips. It was the first time Oscar had ever done a runner.

Of course there was nothing to link the reg of a thieving white Suzuki with a truant Lebanese student from the same college as its owner, but all the same ... And here, up in Tyrone – her idea to fly north, to a separate jurisdiction – his accent would stick out the way her hair was now sticking out. Nothing for it then. With a grunt, he flopped the carcass over with the toe of his boot.

'Shouldn't we wait till it's dark before lighting a fire?' he tried.

She facepalmed her forehead. He nodded slowly, deliberately. 'A fire would be much more visible at night, yeah?' Ok, he thought. You might have won that round baby. And trying to mirror the expression of her eyebrows, he asked 'got any matches, have you?'

There's a saying, you don't know what you have until it's gone. It was much on Oscar's mind as he yanked and ripped and unsnagged moss-upholstered branches from the brambles of the nearest ditch in a race against the failing light. Because if there was one thing he did know, it was that he was gloriously happy. Pretty much from the first moment he'd felt her arms close around his waist and he'd kicked down on the starter, twice, thrice, he'd been filled with the giddy vacancy of a roller coaster ride. He wasn't so young or so skittish as to call it anything but wild infatuation on his part, anything but the expedient of a friend in need on hers, and one who had a motorbike to boot. He hadn't tried anything beyond holding her on either night while they attempted sleep. Besides everything else, she was having her monthlies. All this was a breathless interlude while real life took its course back in the city. The paradox was, he'd never felt so alive.

Dusk was already well advanced before the fire began to take. At that time of year, at these latitudes, the sun, a red dwarf, expires in a tow-coloured west before five o'clock. Winter constellations had begun to shiver above them. It was shaping up to be another cold one. For a long time, her blowing coaxed nothing but tresses of smoke, yellow and choking, from the straw and paper scraps she'd tamped about the kindling. Then in an instant it began to cackle. Soon after, a branch hissed and exploded. All at once the night closed in about them, black and chill. He watched, entranced, the flickering over her complexion, the lynx eyes touched with a glazier's brush. Even the chicken had been alchemised, made almost palatable, quartered and spitted and marinated by the unsteady glow. Already, the portions had begun to sweat and whisper. And he was ravenous. They both were.

IV

She'd eaten far more, and far more recklessly, than he. Cautious, swallowing down waves of sweet saliva, his teeth had torn only the charcoaled exterior, pulled only the charred fibre of thigh muscle, the outer strata from the breast bone. Though they were still temptingly substantial, he'd discarded the joints and the ribcage. She had retrieved them almost before they'd settled.

'Careful with those,' he'd warned her, 'they're not done. You see?' She shrugged, her mouth covered. 'Yasser, that's still pink, it is!' though in the fickle light, this was no more than an educated guess. 'Those black dribbles there, that's blood, surely?'

She shook her hair nest, not even pausing to meet his eye. 'You're such a ...'

Well, now she was paying for it. The winter constellations, Taurus, Orion, the Twins, had wheeled through half the sky and she was still doubled over, heaving and retching intermittently, hacking up gouts of water from a ravaged gut on top of the messy abortion impaled on the hay stubble. She'd been at it for so long that he was more than worried. Three times she'd shrugged off his hand as though it had been responsible for setting it off. Worse, she'd begun to shiver in hard spasms. It was scarcely a surprise; he himself was chilled to the bone. All the same she needed something hot; a black tea; sugared water perhaps; dry toast. Even a blanket would be a help. 'Ok look,' he finally declared. 'I'm going to try that place.' No reply. 'I'll be back, soon as I can, yeah?' She hacked, dribbled, let out a long moan. 'Will you be alright there while I'm gone?' he asked, uselessly.

The farmhouse was a good country mile back along a rough, grass ridged lane. He thought about taking the bike, but decided against it. It would violate the night's sanctity. They were still a pair of fugitives. Who knew what state Gareth Hunt was in by this juncture and whether he'd pressed charges, to say nothing of that fucking Topaz garage. They could have CCTV pictures of his mug splashed all over the papers by now for all he knew.

He became aware of a bone-white gibbous moon riding a far higher arc than the sun had attained. Although the earth was preternaturally still, there must have been stratospheric winds, because rags of indigo cloud were tearing across its eyeball as if in time lapse. Hard not to be reminded of Hunt's class on Buñuel. As he walked the silver-plated laneway he made a mental calculation.

Tuesday, Wednesday. Thursday past midnight, so technically it was already Friday. His dad would be expecting him to ring, especially if he wasn't to head home for the weekend after all. Instinctively, his hand touched his smartphone. It hadn't been turned on since they'd left Kilkenny; her injunction. It tempted. It was all he could do to resist. How many messages were contained there?

On the other hand, he'd an idea that was how they'd trailed the Omagh bombers.

He was running over all this now for the simple reason he had not the foggiest of what to do once he reached the farmhouse. It was coming on for two in the morning. Strange time, at the best of times, to bang on anyone's door. Besides, what was the return to this particular establishment beyond superstition? Late Wednesday evening they'd paused briefly at its barred gate, had peered into the courtyard, a lozenge of wavering light extending over its cobbles. Loud, underwater voices, as from a telly. Could they chance asking for directions, a cuppa, maybe a bite of a sandwich and, top of the list, the use of the loo? There appeared to be a hayloft, perhaps there'd be no objection to them kipping there for the night, two young lovers eloping? *Tír na nÓg* the place was called, carved in the letters of the old script, so chances were the place was Taig, at least there was that to be said for it.

Then she'd pointed out the cat, lodged like a snowdrift on the windowsill. To his mind, the presence of a cat meant it was far less likely there was a psychopathic mongrel on the loose; but to hers that put paid to it. 'Cats give me the creeps,' she'd growled, repeating something she'd confided to him many months before. It wasn't any allergy to cat hairs, or an aversion to their constitutional smugness. Not a bit of it! Had he never noticed the way they shimmy up a wall, defying gravity, slowing into a stride at the top just as if someone had thrown into reverse a projector and run time backwards? That gave her the total heebie-jeebies.

Cat or no cat, Oscar figured *Tír na nÓg* was their best shot now at getting out of the big freeze that had the entire country in its jaws. He'd made the mistake, at the time she'd first explained her cat aversion, of mentioning it to Nigel. They were freshers then, all three of them, and probably it was the kudos of having had the Lebanese beauty confide in him that had incited the indiscretion. They'd sat through one of Hunt's soundless videos the previous week, some experimental arthouse tat that was meant to 'explore the materiality of the celluloid itself as a medium.'

Nigel, of course, guffawed. 'But that's absurd! How can you not like cats for jumping up walls? You might just as well not like kangaroos for the way they skip about the bush.'

'Well? There's some folk hate snakes because they slither. And I hate fucking spiders scurrying about like eight-fingered hands.'

'All the same. A projector running backwards? What planet is she on ...'

'I kind of get it. Do you never get a queasy feeling when they show all the bits of a collapsed chimney or a block of flats climbing back up and fitting in perfectly together, like there was some sort of perfect vacuum at the centre to suck everything into exactly the right place? And she's right: it always rushes upwards, then slows into a freeze, just exactly like a cat shimmying up a wall.'

'But sure, Finn, that's physics! Reversible equations, the top of the parabola, d'you not remember anything out of Titch Toomey's class?'

'Physics my granny. There's more to it. Like when you push a record backwards and you get those Satanic messages. Telling you, I felt queasy all through Hunt's lecture the other week, running things backwards and forwards, backwards and forwards. You can't mess around with time like that.'

Nigel's glasses flashed twin TV screens. 'You're as cracked as she is, Finn. Or she has you that cracked.'

Perhaps it was some trick of the moonlight that appeared to have the courtyard now in suspended animation. All was precisely as it had been in his memory of the previous evening, but silvered, the grasses dyed to black. The lozenge of shimmering light was still there, blues and eerie silvers glimmering across the cobbles. The muffled music was there, incongruously loud. The water barrel was still there, and the hayloft. And now, padding on silent rapid feet, the ghost cat bounced hurriedly toward him, tail erect and stiff as the conducting pole at the back of a bumper car. It gripped Oscar with a tremor of déjà vu.

'Mgrnaaaau!' it said, butting his leg, insistent, aggressively plaintive. 'Mngrnaaaauu!' That, too, was foreseen. But he wasn't the man to back away, not at this point. Too much had gone down in the last few days. If she could be a warrior, damn it, so could he.

He tugged the bolt on the gate, slipped a twine loop, allowed gravity swing it open. He shivered once, took a stride forwards, the cat bounding ahead of him like a white familiar. It was only when he had reached the window and saw what was inside that he froze.

PART TWO

I

Yasmin Hasan was huddled at the embers looking moody and ravaged. She squinted up at him. Orange-lit from below, the half moons under her eyes made her almost haggard, her hair straggled and specked with hay, a seer from the Dark Ages. Her voice was weak, not quite abashed, but in the same territory. 'So did you get something?'

He searched for words. A plethora of versions had tumbled around his head on the quick trek back, none of them adequate. 'You got to see this for yourself, Yaz! It's totally ... *weird*. Like something out of David Lynch, I swear to you.' Her eyes hadn't moved from his. 'Come on, I'll show you!' He lifted up her backpack, scarcely bigger than a schoolbag. 'Yaz, you need to come with me.'

He'd expected her to protest. He'd expected at the least that she'd demand some sort of justification. Instead she rose up, hunched against the night, and allowed him to manoeuvre her toward the lane. 'Can we take the bike?' she pleaded. And, when he'd relented and pulled the Suzuki and helmets from their hiding place – 'I never want to see a chicken again as long as I live.'

They scrambled awkwardly along the lane, not so much because of the potholes as because she was slumped against him. Her inertia forced him to take each bend gingerly, his boot sole scraping over the surface. He stopped the bike just short of the final bend and, helping her off, angled it onto its stand. 'It's only round the corner,' he assured her, heart beating at the unexpected reversal of roles.

The gate was open, just as he'd left it. The light was still playing eerily over the cobbles. TV sounds, bass and conspicuous, pulsed about the courtyard. There was a high whine, a dog locked in somewhere. Rapidly, as though the frames of a film were playing at an accelerated speed, tail erect, the cat padded toward them. 'Fuck off! Fuck off!' she hissed down at it, but without real conviction, hoisting rather than kicking it to one side with her boot. The food poisoning had taken more than just the chicken out of her. The cat was not so easily discouraged, and leaned again into the boot, so Oscar scooped up its heft and deposited it in one deft movement atop the wall, its pelt buffing the miniature ribcage. 'Mngrnnaauuu!' it protested.

They'd barely entered the courtyard when a cramp took her. 'Uggghh!' she doubled. He allowed her a moment. 'I swear to god, Oscar, if I ever hear so much as a cluck ...'

What to say? Anything he could think of seemed to either smack of 'I told you so' or, so deliberately did it avoid doing so, the lacuna seemed to imply it. So he smiled, unseen, then edged toward the farmhouse. When she hadn't moved to follow he returned, kneaded her shoulders, then guided her toward the windowsill. 'You've got to see this for yourself, Yaz.'

Every circuit in his body came alive with static when, in her weakness, she subsided against him, her hair smelling of smoke and damp and tallow. He positioned her by the shoulders to face the interior. 'You see what I'm saying?' he gasped. Because the scene through the window was precisely as he had left it a half hour before to run back for her: the submarine light playing all around the room, distending shadows, turning it into an aquarium, and washing again and again over a figure slumped by the dead hearth, head down and mouth agape.

'What am I supposed to be looking at?' she whispered.

For a second he was baffled 'you *do* see that guy?'

He felt her shrug, so? 'Ok here's the thing. I watched him for about five minutes earlier on. Then I tapped at the window. Nothing. I tried slapping it. Not a squeak! So then I banged at the door. Same story.' He paused. She was leaning back against him, head lolling, eyes, at a guess, closed tight. 'So maybe he's deaf,' she breathed out.

'*Deaf*?' He hadn't considered the possibility; could that be why the volume was turned up full? No. *No*. 'Dead would be nearer the mark!' And as if to prove a point, he slapped at the window so forcefully that its membrane vibrated like a drum's. 'Halloo!' he called, making a bullhorn out of his left hand. 'Anyone home?'

Yasmin had slid away and materialised at the door, but far from knocking on it she'd thumbed the latch and was leaning into the doorway, edging it open, releasing the full volume of the television into the courtyard. The cat rippled past her and was gone inside.

'What are you at!? Jesus, you can't just go ...'

Already from the interior, 'I'm dying for the loo,' called a voice that would brook neither delay nor dissension.

Ten minutes passed. There was still no sign of her emerging. 'Oh for feck sake!' he muttered, teeth clenched. Some minutes before, a fluent discharge in an exterior pipe had suggested a toilet flush. Anticipation had then gradually given way to frustration. The only other sound, above the din of the television, was a persistent whining and occasional rush of scratches at an outhouse door; a dog locked in a shed somewhere. Twice he glanced around, as if help or encouragement might be found there. 'Well feck this anyway!' he hissed again, then made through the tentative entrance.

From the very first step, it felt like transgression. The interior was loud, stale, unreal. Shadows stretched and flittered about the walls and over the flagstones like dark insubstantial flames. Incongruous, flippant music was booming out of the television. His eyes on the corpse – for surely it was a lifeless thing – he edged toward the interior doorway. 'Yasser!' he called, muting his voice lest it disturb the cadaver. 'Hi, Yaz?'

Briefly, he peered into the deaf hallway. Across the carpet poured a rhomboid of yellow light. He nodded in the direction of the dead man as though apologising, then sidled by touch toward it. Curiously, he had dismissed the thought that in the bungalow there might live a second inhabitant. He backed as far as the open doorway and glanced into what he knew would be a bedroom. There she lay, booted, jacketed, face down across the duvet, head in the crook of her arm, from the corner of her mouth to her thumb a fine thread of drool. She hadn't even removed the backpack.

He extinguished the light, tiptoed out, closed over the door. Then he went back to the living room and, examining for a spell the washes of light over the waxen face and scalp, he turned down rather than muted the television. Some piety held him from turning it off entirely, or from changing the channel. On a plate at the foot of the chair, set by the dead hearth, the cat was savaging the carcass of a meal.

He tiptoed into the kitchenette, turned the tap, and drank greedily at the icy water that stuttered out of it. Then he retraced his steps, closed the outer door and rattled it to be sure it was secure. He then sat, back to the wall of the tiny hallway, in a dream-haunted vigil, the head jerking upright after each gradual subsiding. If anyone were to chance upon the house, a relative, say, it wouldn't do at all to find the two intruders sleeping in the bed.

II

He was up and about long since, foostering through the exterior sheds to baffle the growls of his hunger, when she finally appeared in the doorway. Barefoot, t-shirt and jeans, stretching blithely as an animal. It was past eleven. 'Hi Alpha Nerd,' she waved, 'any chance you could figure how to get the shower working?' He squinted at the apparition. 'Are you serious?' Her silence said it all. He was an idiot. 'Very well!' he said, tossing down an axe he'd encountered. 'I'll see what I can do.'

Following her inside, he was surprised to find the TV screen dead, the kitchenette in disarray, two press doors open, sundry items on the counter by the sink. 'What were you doing in here?' he asked, eyes hovering now over the slumped man.

She shrugged. 'Trying to make us porridge. Then the electricity went, paff!'

Doubtfully he eyed the kettle, the open pack of Flahavan's beside it. Two bowls, with spoons in them, something from a cautionary fairytale; tea leaves like ants or grains of gunpowder trailing to an open caddy; a collapsed sugar bag. He shut his eyes and watched the darkness spark. Best not to think. 'You must have tripped a fuse,' he offered.

'So come on then, fix it, Mr Nerd.'

'Let me find the box first, would you?'

Even though he was ravenous, even though the dead man could have no possible use for the open packets, it did not sit easy with him that she'd riffled the interior of his cupboards. And she was being so bloody nonchalant about the whole thing, almost sing song! Ach, his scruples were silly, no doubt. The result of insomnia and fraught nerves. Two further considerations held him from picking her up on it. Number one, she must be even more ravenous than he, having emptied her guts several times over the night before. And number two, an hour since, he'd carried out a first, albeit tiny, disobedient act. He'd had a sneaky check of his phone messages.

How long would it need to be on, he'd reasoned, before they got a fix on it? After all, he wasn't about to make a call out. Not even 171. And they were only a dozen miles across the border, not even. That was hardly enough for Vodaphone UK, or whatever they had up here, to kick in. Besides, was there any reason they'd be interested in the whereabouts of this particular phone, even if they had connected it to the theft of a tank of petrol outside of Kilkenny; even if they had in some manner linked that tank of petrol to the flight of Yasmin Hasan from the college? Seriously, what were the chances?

All the same he'd limited it to the briefest of surveys. He weighed the device for a minute, scrutinised the kitchen window to see if there was any sign she was up and about, then ignited it. It kicked like a live creature. Three messages and a missed call, all from Nigel. In order of date, the messages were 'R u meant 2 b thelma r louise?'; 'Ring!' and 'Get in touch cant u', no apostrophe. There was also a voicemail. Before he could commit himself to checking it, his thumb had extinguished the phone.

The fuse box wasn't hard to locate and he flicked up the thrown switch. Instantly, the TV burst back to life. The kettle gave a low gurgle, the water reconfiguring. 'Yay!' she called. From the fuse box he moved quickly to the bathroom, tugged at a string, saw a red light blink on. She slid by him with irony and pushed him out the door. He heard the shower stutter into life, then heard her voice, muffled and feminine. 'Hoy! Get a fire going, lover mine. It's Baltic out there.'

Grand, so. Chopping wood would at the least afford him another opportunity *not* to think. When first he'd woken fully out of his fitful vigil at the back door, he'd tiptoed in as far as the bedroom and edged the door. She was under the duvet now but for two limbs, still as a centrefold; on the floor the boots empty and askew, the knapsack still hugging the collapsed jacket like a koala, the jeans pulled inside out alongside them. He'd stood for a transgressively long time, the vision a part of the unreality of insomnia, but a gorgeous part of it. Then he'd eased the action of the door handle and tiptoed out past the dead man, head angled so as not to allow his presence enter beyond the periphery of vision, and left the house.

At that time, he had who knew how much time to kill and little purposeful activity with which to kill it. There were too many questions, scruples and apprehensions haunting the recesses to allow him simply enjoy the escapade. Now at least there was wood to be chopped. Feeling vaguely ludicrous, he set his feet apart, spat into his palms, then drove the axe into a stump where it instantly stuck fast. It took him much effort with foot and both arms and quite a few obscenities before it squeaked free. The third stroke sent a wicked shiver up through the haft that struck the bones of his hand like a blow. Fuck this for a game of soldiers! There was one outhouse he had yet to check, the one from which, even now, the high whines of the dog were emanating, thinner than before. Perhaps it was a coal shed. Why not? The hearth in front of which the dead man was slumped had been grey with ash. He had to have burned something in it.

Oscar attended to the whining, high and plaintiff and interrupted by a desperate snuffling in proportion as he approached. Would it be a vicious bastard? Probably, though possibly it was merely starving. The cat had fair torn into that plate of scraps and bones that the old man had set down by the fire. Besides, Oscar had found a nest of bloodied feathers earlier where it had presumably ambushed a bird of some kind. But a dog locked into a shed? At the very least it must be parched. Who knew how long the old man had been slumped there? But could he chance letting it out? A cat, at least, wouldn't savage you.

Briefly, he was put in mind of a jingle his father, that shy man, would recite as a party piece:

Edward Carson had a cat, it sat upon the fender
And every time the fire spat the cat cried 'No Surrender!'

She wouldn't get it, though. A pity. Too much exegesis required; the old man-killing parishes and all that. Great hatred, little room. 'Wait a minute!' he said, aloud. 'Wait just one minute!' In his mind's eye beside the plate of scraps the cat had ravished there'd stood a bucket. A few old bricks of turf, rough-hewn as though dug from a bog. There *had* been, hadn't there? He threw down the axe, marched back toward the house, ignored the cascade of scraping that assaulted the door of the shed. Well feck it, if they *were* to stay till after they'd breakfasted, they might just as well be warm! It was just a case of manoeuvring the old man's chair away from the fireplace.

For the first time he examined the body at close quarters. In the daylight it was ashen, incontrovertibly lifeless. The air about it was charged with an odour of decrepitude, faint but persistent. It was the mouldy cardboard waft he associated with charity shops, but underlain by something more offensive, too. The mouth was agape, toothless, rimed with spittle. The eyes, half-closed, were two glass beads, a child's attempt to express country slyness. The pate was mottled like a trout and faintly scabbed, giving way to abrupt brown ridges where it met the weather-beaten forehead as though two distinct complexions had been clumsily grafted together. He resisted the instinct to tamp down the wisps of a white corona. 'Well, old timer,' said Oscar. To move the chair without a single word seemed a breach of etiquette. In protest against the grain of the drag, the body juddered rigidly.

He was still involved in the painstaking manoeuvre when herself arrived, a bath towel dangling from her chest to her middle thigh. With another, she'd begun to pat out the magnificent tendrils of her hair. Simultaneously, Oscar was host to a throb of desire and a prickly sensation at the inappropriateness both of her state of undress and of his throb. Framed in the doorway she looked from him to the empty grate, still cold with unswept ash.

'Tell me, have you ever seen a corpse, Oscar?'

'I have actually,' he said, in reflex. His abrupt tone meant he now had to follow it up, to lay at her feet a fact. 'I saw my Mam's. The Da threw a wake for her when she passed on. I must have been ten at a guess.' When she didn't reply he heard himself add, as though by way of apology, 'She'd been sick for the longest time.'

She was surprised. Not impressed, surprised. It struck him how little she knew about him, how little curiosity he'd ever elicited. 'What did she look like?'

'What did she *look* like?' Both hands still on the back of the chair, he considered. 'You mean, after ...' What was the word?

'Yep. After.'

'I remember,' the memory, unreal, shadowy, underexplored, would gain in reality as he now gave it words. 'I remember a house filled with whispers.' That wasn't it. 'I remember being stuffed into a blue suit, and then all these poshly-dressed grown ups shaking my hand like I was a grown up too.' That wasn't it, either. 'But what I remember most, can you guess?' She waited for him to go on. 'I'm not surprised. What I remember most are the bursts of frivolity. Boisterous, uneasy frivolity. "God rest her," declared my father, his hand at the head of the coffin, "but she wouldn't begrudge us a laugh." Hey, you do know there's a law in Ireland says no one is allowed to be buried until such time as someone says sure they wouldn't begrudge us a laugh?'

'Yeah, but what did she look like?'

He stared at her, not understanding.

'Had she been prettified?'

'Mam?' He lived again the dark scent of mahogany and polish so powerful it was a taste, the hand at his shoulder ushering him forward to peer over the fluted edge. 'She looked like a dummy out of a waxworks. Only, I remember thinking at the time it wasn't a particularly good likeness.'

She thought about this for a minute, processed it. 'You see, Oscar, I've seen plenty of corpses. Old, young. *Not* prettified,' she stressed, her eyebrows hoisting then dropping, a semaphore for QED. Her point made, the subject was closed. He could stop pussyfooting with the chair and get on with setting the fire.

III

It was she who'd released the dog. After the turf had begun to settle in the grate, after the porridge, after the milk-less tea and her determinedly loud inventory of the cupboards and freezer (nothing at all could be salvaged out of the fridge's sour exhalation), she'd bundled his reluctance toward the shower.

'No, I wouldn't feel right about it, Yaz.'

'Yeah? Well let me tell you something, mister, you're beginning to stink worse than the stiff, you know that?'

The *stiff*, Christ! 'So what am I supposed to use for a towel?'

'They're at the top of the hot press. If you *wouldn't feel right about that*,' she trumped his delicacy, 'you can use the same ones I used,' at which the wet towel was slapped peremptorily around his face.

To be fair to her, the shower was glorious. It steamed at the very threshold of pain, so scalding it froze his skin. It refreshed like a good evacuation or an hour of deepest sleep, set his spirits soaring. He even found himself singing, had to stop abruptly out of respect for the deceased. By the time he was outside and towelling his head against the frosty air, she'd freed the dog, a mongrel three-fourths border collie with one eye dark, one agate. A wolf's eye. It slunk toward him in a craven, suspicious arc, hair bunched on its shoulders like a fur stole. 'He doesn't bite,' she called, brightly.

'Oh yeah?'

'I was talking to the dog!'

'Oh, ha ha!' He made to go back inside, to finish drying himself.

'Listen, can you get your RTÉ up here?'

His RTÉ. He shrugged *I guess.*

'What time is their news meant to be on, anyhow?'

'One,' he said, not at all relishing the lack of courtesy that fiddling the dead man's channel would entail. All the same, it was as well to know how things stood down in Dublin.

That evening they had their first falling out. From the news at one and again at six, it was clear that Gareth Hunt remained in intensive care, his injuries serious but not life-threatening. For more than thirty six hours he'd remained in a coma. That silence took them only to Thursday morning and it was now Friday evening. Still nothing, beyond the definite line of inquiry the Gardaí were pursuing. Neither names nor photographs enlivened the brief report. Had the man spoken, or was he still too heavily sedated? Maybe the wanker thought better of dragging up anything suspect involving one of his students. But the point was, they didn't know. He might be playing games with her. For all they knew the guards might be playing games with her.

Nigel would know the score.

'I'm sorry, did you say *Nigel*?'

'Whatever you might think about him, he'd have his ear to the ground on this one.'

'Yeah if he could let go of the Xbox for long enough he might!'

'Why not ask him? What's to lose? He texted me to say to ...' She stared. Too late, he realised his mistake. 'Yeah, I checked my texts earlier. Hey, I only had the phone on for twenty seconds. Twenty seconds max.' Stony silence. 'I didn't make any calls out, ok?'

She looked at him as if he'd just slapped her across the face and was now coolly deciding whether it was worth her while to exterminate him. 'You texted him,' she said, at length.

'No. I told you. *He* texted *me*. I just read them, is all.'

Frost descended on the room. If there was one thing that Oscar Finn couldn't abide, it was the silent treatment. His stepmum had medals for it. So his thoughts raced around the four walls, desperate to light upon an idea, any idea. Instead they lighted upon the phone. A landline! He sat up and clacked his fingers. 'I've got it! How about I *do* call him and ask what's up,' he waved his smartphone, a decoy, 'only I use your man's phone?'

'Yeah that's brilliant, Oscar.'

'Why not?' In the smouldering absence of a reply he tried to imagine one. Because they had a trace on Nigel's number? But that was patently ludicrous. Perhaps even now she was realising the same thing. She rose. She left the room. 'Do what you like for all I care,' she sighed from the doorframe.

Later, he found her sitting by the gate, one of the farmer's caps aslant on her head. His impulse was to admonish her for the breach of common decency. On the other hand, she looked ridiculously sexy. She was toying with the collie, cuffing it, pushing its head from side to side while it pawed her thigh excitedly. *Not* looking at him. At some distance the cat watched, totem still, wary of the girl rather than the dog. 'Yeah, so I spoke to Nige.'

'And?'

'And nothing. He was more interested in the big question as to whether I'd got my end away!'

She almost allowed a smile. 'So what did you tell him?'

'I assured him my celibacy was intact.' He was on the point of adding 'regrettably', but he didn't want to push the thaw too far. 'For what it's worth, the rumour mill has you fighting Hunt off with the helmet.' Pause. 'They're all sure it was you.'

She seemed disinterested. 'Yeah?'

'Yeah. They figure it must've been a student seeing how it happened in his office and nothing was taken. I mean, nothing bar the helmet. Oh yeah, the word around college is it happened that evening, not eleven o'clock. So I guess that means either Hunt hasn't said anything, or if he did, he let on about the time.' There'd been a question churning in his gut for three days now. 'Can I ask you, what was the story with you guys in first year anyhow?' Another hiatus, while she nuzzled and repulsed the collie with its one domestic, one atavistic iris. 'I mean, were you seeing each other or what?'

'Hunh!' she snorted. 'He tried it on enough times, that's for sure.' Then she stood, made for the gate, and clicked 'Come on boy!'

Later again, his compunction was once more disturbed. They were getting ready for an early night. 'I'm not at all sure about kipping in the man's bed, Yaz.'

'Yeah? So go kip in a haystack if it makes you feel better.'

'It's just, you know ...'

If she did know, she wasn't showing it. She was sitting on the bed, he hovering at the threshold. She'd already zipped off her boots and now, in full view, she peeled the jeans down her legs and kicked them inside out onto a chair he had no memory of seeing before. She must have dragged in from the kitchen expressly. 'So?' she said.

'So,' he shrugged. All at once, as if from extreme fatigue, his resistance subsided. Two minutes later, in boxers, in darkness, he shuffled under the duvet against her. He resumed the same hugging position as on previous nights, pressed into her back, knees folded under hers. But on previous nights, they'd been fully dressed. Through her light t-shirt her body radiated animal heat. His erection was patent as an exclamation mark. When she'd felt its presence she'd guffawed.

Several eternal minutes passed. He could sense that her eyes were open. So, by slow degrees, he attempted to alter the meaning of the embrace. Tentatively, he drew gentle circles on her bicep with his thumb, just under the gap where the sleeve ended. After a while, when that had raised no protest, he planted a light kiss at the nape of the neck. No response. But then, no discouragement, either.

He could both feel and hear his own hot breath blowing over her skin. After about thirty iterations he chanced a light nibble on the shoulder. 'Don't,' she said, with the barest stiffening. Later, though, she intertwined his fingers. He read the gesture to include the possibility that what she'd meant had been 'don't, yet.'

IV

The next day, Saturday, the waft of decrepitude was palpable. It had aroused the lethargy of a housefly. All day it remained, stupefied by winter, a lewd raison congealed at the corner of the nether lip. Unable to convince her to resume the road while the sun was still feebly shining, Oscar spent as much of the day as he could away from the house.

The tool shed in which the dog had been confined was a mausoleum inside which time had grown old. Once the door's arthritic hinges had been ratcheted open, the interior smelled of rust and spores, of axle grease and damp masonry. The shelves were crowded with ancient paint tins; with yellowed plastic tubs of screws, nails, and washers; with oxidised cans and boxes in faded labels from another age. Through cracks, long wax-white tendrils had probed the blind interior. There was a roughly-built wooden table with a vice grip, there was a clutter of broomsticks and handles with a bizarre assortment of time-encrusted heads. High up was a tiny window filmed over with cataracts of dust and filament, and in every corner hung opaque nests of milky cobweb that were nightmares of insect wings and disarticulated limbs. It made a passable hideaway for the bike and helmets.

That done, Oscar passed the chief of the day scouting the fields, getting a sense, as he would tell her if she asked, of the lay of the land. What he was really about was getting a sense of their escapade, and of this foreign woman who'd initiated it – he could no longer think of her as a girl merely. Under his leathers his jumper was itching him. She'd cajoled him to handwash his under-things, after which she'd hung them outside. He'd reluctantly consented to borrow a pair of the old man's socks, but he drew the line at the baggy y-fronts and vest she'd set out for him on the bed. With his crotch, too, he had to be careful while he stalked the frozen fields.

One curiosity. The dog wouldn't go with him. It slunk along, stirring its tail in slow motion, but only as far as the first corner. Beyond this it would not venture. It had formed too strong a bond with its liberator, she who gave it scraps to eat and played roughly with its adoration. On the other hand, it would not enter the house. Perhaps this inhibition dated back to the old regime, but Oscar couldn't help but think that the misgiving was aroused by the whiff of putrefaction that tainted the air. The cat showed no such compunction and trotted blithely about the place, mewling up to Yasmin's constitutional antipathy, recovering quickly and stubbornly from each and every rebuff.

Musing upon the cat, playing variations on the theme, he considered the bizarre aetiology of her loathing. Nige maintained it was one of the great conundrums of physics, why time's arrow pointed in one direction only. But did it? Was it not rather our awareness of time that ran in one direction only, like a record moving under a needle? Perhaps the Great Chronologer played with time like a DJ scratching a disc forward and back, forward and back. If consciousness runs one way only, how would we know the difference? With no absolute against which to measure or calibrate, every occasion wouldn't just seem the first occasion, it *would be* the first occasion. Wind back the clock, our knowledge of what was to come would unwind too. Several times, in several formulations, he'd put that argument to his flatmate, who in his exasperating manner did that trick with his left eyebrow to suggest superiority and promptly changed the subject or the channel.

Yet in his gut Oscar empathised with her misgiving. There was some ontic absurdity in Humpty Dumpty rising from the dust and spontaneously slowing back together again that provoked queasiness. Now, at some point in space/time, there had been a catastrophic convergence of Gareth Hunt's motorbike helmet and his skull from which the latter had come off the worse. If she could rewind that particular reel, would she? He doubted it. And what about Oscar? That Topaz garage, say. Because the point was this, even though it had been done on the spur of the moment, yet there had been an instant calculation behind the lie. At the level of instinct, or reflex, some shrewder spur had impelled him to take the step that could not be taken back. Not exactly Cortes burning the ships, but it committed him to the adventure. It set him on a course that was parallel to hers.

Of course he'd known, even as he'd muttered 'no, no petrol', that this wasn't so. Doing a runner from a garage was scarcely on a par with leaving a lecturer stretched out unconscious. For god's sake it wasn't even irreversible. A squaring of the bill and an apology for the oversight and chances were the whole misadventure would be duly forgotten. *Went clean out of my head, I don't know what I was thinking. You're grand, son, sure it happens every day of the week, we'll say no more about it.* She could hardly say the like to Gareth Hunt, even if she had a mind to.

He found that he'd come to the very barn where, two evenings previously, she'd stunned the bird with a single shot. He moved to the doorway as if to verify that the incident had actually taken place. The white sun, which all day had scarcely cleared the hedgerows, cast long and well-defined shadows, turning the floor into a moonscape of muck and cowpats. He entered, smiled wanly at the childishness of the trap he'd set. There was a rumour of wings in the rafters, pigeons probably. One corner had a dozen bales of hay. If she'd agree to leave the house they could do worse than hole up here for the night. But what were the chances? Three times already he'd hinted they were bound to be discovered in that infernal farmhouse.

A thought took him. The door of the tool shed had been stiff, the hinges rusted and misaligned. He'd had to force them in order to wobble it shut, and then had to hoist the door so the bolt would slide in. Everything about it declared its lack of use. So how came the dog to be locked in there?

Oscar hunkered down, the better to pursue the thought. Did the old man shut the dog in there every night? There was nothing in the interior to suggest it; no bowl or dish; no lead; no receptacle for water. Nor had he noticed any dog hairs. So had it been a one off? A punishment? A precaution, because poison had been put down in one of the fields hereabouts? Perhaps the animal had taken a hen.

But it didn't appear the kind of dog that would take a hen. Too ... *domesticated*, notwithstanding the mismatched eyes. It must have been pretty much starving by the time she'd released it, but it had taken any scrap that Yasmin had offered it with a gentle mouth.

And that was another point, how long precisely had it been locked in there?

Earlier in the day he'd made a half-assed attempt to gauge how long the old man had been dead. Overnight the body had slumped in the chair, and was nowhere as stiff as when he'd first moved it stutteringly from the fireplace. He'd loathed going anywhere near it, and held his breath till his lungs clamoured against the proximity of decomposition. He'd decided to examine the stubble. There was nothing, of course, to say that the man had shaved on the day of his death, but what you could say with certainty was that he hadn't been next or near a razor since then! Rather than touch the corpse with its grotesque housefly, Oscar had tipped the chair backwards on its legs until the head lolled back and rolled, the fish gape exhaling a horrible bubble of gas that all but had him gagging. The jowl, marbled like beef, was hoared over now, a fine stubble glistering and erect like a field of filings tickled by a magnet. But its metallic presence seemed to have as much to do with the watery light streaming in through the window as from any actual growth. Beneath the jaw was a longer, soft white down, untouched by a razor.

Ach, who was he kidding? He was no forensic scientist.

A new thought took him as he crouched by the trap. What precisely had killed the old man? A stroke? A heart attack? Possibly. But suppose it hadn't been he who had locked the dog in the shed. Suppose it had been an intruder. Say an autopsy were to show that he'd been suffocated and then dragged into that chair, they could tell that sort of thing. And then say they found the two of them, still squatting there, three days later. What was to say they hadn't done the old man in?

But if it had been an intruder who'd locked away the dog, what possible motive was there? There'd been no sign of a burglary, of anything having been rifled. Unless, of course, the supposed assailant had known precisely what they were looking for, and where to find it. A relative, say; a wayward son who'd wanted to destroy a will that cut him out of the inheritance.

No. It was too far-fetched. It was something himself and Nigel might have dreamed up as a film script before Nige had become a CGI nerd and general pain-in-the-arse. All the same, if he could think of how to give it maximum leverage, he might use the thought to coax herself away from that accursed farmhouse.

And then? That was the crux of the matter. That was the question that three days of biking and running and hiding and shivering and embracing her electric proximity had allowed him to evade. And then? Addressing those two innocent words was the real purpose of his present wanderings. Because at one level, it was far easier for her to answer 'and then?' In her case, it was largely a geographical question. She'd mentioned catching the boat to Scotland. She had no family here; therefore, she had no responsibilities, here. There was a brother in France she scarcely spoke of, parents who were separated and who weren't even living in the same country. No, Yasmin Hasan was free, and being free had made her a free spirit.

All the same, her insensitivity about the old man's body had taken him aback. It bothered him far more than the fact of her having fetched Gareth Hunt such a clatter that he'd ended up in the ICU. Funny, that lack of courtesy should trouble him far more than violence. It was how he'd been raised. Theirs was a quiet house, his old man a shy individual overshadowed by Oscar's stepmum. That, too, was part of the crux, because if he was to look 'what then?' square in the eye, if he was to say to 'what then?' I'm going to live to the full this road movie that has been thrust upon me, then he'd have to deal with the matter of his father.

More companions than sweethearts, his real parents had married, finally, only after the mother's diagnosis, on foot of it perhaps. And the old man was already the wrong side of fifty when Oscar had been born. A late pregnancy, unexpected. Unwise. None of his school friends had folks so elderly. At parent teacher meetings, Oscar had been aware of the discrepancy to the point of embarrassment. When he was seven or eight, to his shame, he'd remained silent when Dots O'Leary had asked were they his grandparents awaiting him at the school gate.

If he were to leave, now, on a whim ... but damn it all, it wasn't the 1950s or 60s! There wasn't the slow haemorrhage of the young you'd see on *Reeling in the Years*, the lost generation who'd left behind a country of old men. These days you Skyped, you flew home for long weekends. And it wasn't as if his old man would object to him dropping out of a course he never entirely saw the point of.

As for herself ...

The stepmother had come into their household when Oscar was eleven. She was eighteen years younger than his dad, an efficient woman not much given to laughing. There'd been none of that hostility you might hear about, the stranger displacing the idealised image of the dead mother. No new sibling was forthcoming to displace him, and was hardly likely to now she was well beyond childbearing age. Nor had she arrived with any visible baggage from her previous marriage. But from the first, they'd got off to a bad start.

It was a question of awkwardness rather than resentment, on her part too. For the simple fact was, Oscar Finn never knew how to address the woman. Mother or

Mum was simply wrong. Sandra was too familiar. Mrs Cummins was obsolete with the marriage. Oscar had fallen on the expedient of never actually addressing her by name, instead supplying a cough or an 'em' as required. She was aware of this, and she let him know she was aware of it. She eyed him with an air of mild irony, he the perpetually gauche perpetual adolescent. It was an expression that would alter not a jot when she heard her stepson had taken flight.

Oscar shivered. The light, what was left of it, was cold. It was time to head back. Besides, he was ravenous. Time enough for scruples after they'd eaten.

V

Their second falling out was more serious than the first.

When he got back within sight of the farm the lights were on, the glow butter-coloured. At the gate, the dog slunk out of the evening and nosed his hand. The agate eye, and *Tír na nÓg* in runic letters. Not for the first time, Oscar was seized with a feeling of déjà vu, as though he'd caught at last the Great Chronologer scratching the record back and forth, back and forth. Or maybe he was what's-his-name Guy Pearce in *Momento*, forever reliving the same screenplay.

The table was already laid. Turf was glowing and greying in the grate. He could have scripted that, too. He pulled off his boots, caked in winter mud, then held his breath against the fetor while he crossed reverently to the sink to wash his hands. Yasmin observed his actions with an amused irony uncomfortably close to that of his stepmum. It was not an analogy he was prepared to entertain.

She was no great shakes as a cook, that much was apparent. All the same, his delicious hunger had already wolfed the conglomerate of sweetcorn, spaghetti hoops and fish fingers before he noticed the trove in his dessert bowl: coins of brass and silver over a few bizarre looking notes. He tipped it out, slid the coins into corresponding piles. The total, with the notes, came to just shy of thirty pounds. He looked at her warily.

'Came across it in a biscuit tin,' she shrugged. When he said nothing to this, she added. 'We've no other sterling, my love.'

He dragged the hoard back into the bowl, pushed it to one side, sniffed, rubbed his eyes. His own voice sounded foreign to him, quiet, viscous with phlegm. 'I'm surprised,' he said, 'you didn't try his trouser pockets while you were at it.' She looked right at him, her smirk cancelling out a tone he'd tried to lace with sarcasm. Her arm extended across the table, the fingers opening singly, like petals. In the palm, a miraculous medal and a scapular of the Sacred Heart.

'You didn't! For Christ's sake,' he muttered, his breath unsteady. For a while he considered the mockery on her brow. 'Ok. *You'll* say he can't possibly have any use for the cash, am I right? Maybe so. But I got to tell you, Yaz, I don't feel right about any of this, you know?' Her expression hadn't changed one iota, the lynx eyes, the amused brow. 'Ok. Suppose his family were to discover us here (yeah?), with your man sitting there god knows how long at this stage. What are they going to think?' The question hung heavy above them, a limp flag, unsaluted. He began to feel angry. 'I'll tell you what they'll think. They'll think we're a pair of monsters. And maybe they wouldn't be too far wrong.'

'So what are you proposing? Hey, you want to phone the police, the phone is right there mister! There's no one stopping you.'

Check. He to play. He looked at it, a prosthetic-coloured piece, as though the answer to her challenge might be somehow inscribed there. He took a deep breath. 'Look

I've been thinking, Yasmin. Suppose we go back to Dublin?'

'Hunh! And do what?'

'I mean, what's the worst that can happen?' Her stare suggested that it was obvious. 'Even if Hunt was to tell the guards it was you hit him, you could argue self defence. I mean, the man was way out of line. He's the one should be running scared, not you.'

'I'm out of the college, pal. Forget the guards!' She exhaled, hotly. 'Ok, let me spell it out for you. No college, no visa.' Her delivery was becoming vicious. 'You ever spent the night in a sleeping bag queuing on Burgh Quay?'

'Hunh!' he snorted.

She wasn't prepared to let the question be rhetorical. 'Well? Have you?'

'There's other colleges, Yaz.'

'Yeah right. They're going to take me in with my references?'

'Hold on. Think, a minute. They're going to expel you? Not a chance! More likely Hunt is facing the heave-ho. Think about it for a minute. The media would have a field day with this particular baby! A college lecturer (right?), calls a student into his office at half ten at night, then tries it on with her ...?'

For a minute she stared at him, as if assessing his trustworthiness, or else his stupidity. 'Who said he tried it on?'

The six words struck him with the force of a blow, winding him. When he'd at last drawn breath, he whispered 'Jesus, Yasmin, what are you saying to me?'

Silence, broken only by the tumble of ashes in the grate. All at once the dusk seemed to have thickened in the unlit room, become tangible; in it, under it, the sweet, disgusting spoor of decomposition. Now it was a house of ticks and groans, the furniture as if recalibrating. In the half-light, only her eyes retained their lustre. 'He told me he was failing me.'

Oscar shook his head, an invitation to go on. But he was aware, even as he listened, that there were crosscurrents tugging laterally inside him. He sensed he was working quite deliberately now toward a showdown; that the outburst, when it came, would be less than honest. Her words had stunned him, yes. But there was something of his own in the mix. Foreboding? Guilt?

Any trace of amusement had been wiped from her brow. He found himself gazing at it. Another curiosity: when she frowned, her forehead never became corrugated; rather it puckered lightly, a breeze playing upon water. 'Alright,' she said. 'So there was this chunk of the dissertation he said I'd cut and pasted straight from the web. He'd underlined it in red. Twice. Put a box around it, in case it might somehow slip away I suppose. The fucker refused to look at me, just tossed back the dissertation as if it had dirt on it. When he did speak, he was talking to the window, or more accurately straight to his smug reflection. "You are going down, my friend".' As she quoted him, her eyes glared like headlights.

'And had you?' She hadn't understood. 'Taken it from the web?'

She shook her head, but not as a denial; rather, she was dismissing the query. 'He knew what he was doing. That *fucker* knows exactly what going down means where I'm concerned. Haha! Call it revenge if you want. "*You* are going down, my friend" Oscar, you want to have heard the way the bastard said it.'

'But how much *had* you taken off the web?' He examined her pupils, which seemed to have distilled what little light was left in the room. When they tried to flick away he held them. In slow motion she shook her head. 'Everyone copies from the web. And don't you dare tell me you've never done it either.'

He was too busy digesting the thought that Gareth Hunt hadn't gone near her to reply that he hadn't. Still nervous with her revelation, still feeling the strong crosscurrent that was threatening to drag him under, he wasn't ready to let it go. He felt his thigh pumping up and down, so that the calmness of his tone surprised him. 'Yes, but how much, Yaz? That's the point here.' To break the interrogation, she stood, took the plates to the bin, scraped them noisily, angrily. 'Fuck you,' she said.

That was it. The damn burst. 'Yeah?' His right hand was shaking so violently he had actually to sit on it to keep it quiet. 'So anyone stands in your way, you just send them to intensive care, that it?'

'Yeah. That's it!'

'Feck sake! You don't even ...' With his free arm, his left, he gestured widely toward the body of the old man, slumped and stupid. Some force was impelling him once more to take the step that couldn't be taken back. There was another current, even deeper. A wilder current, dangerous as a riptide. And he, Oscar, sensed that he was forcing a breach with her because he couldn't face how full-on crazy he was about her. Probably she sensed it, too. When she spoke, it was with deathly calm. 'So why don't you fuck off back to Dublin?'

'Maybe I will.'

She tossed back her hair, guffawed, pronounced with understated derision the verdict: 'Mama's boy.' It was so perfect that Oscar Finn actually laughed. That's how much his presence had meant to her! Had she even *heard* him say that at ten years of age he'd been present at his mother's wake?

A minute extended, a second. It would have been impossible to say if the silence was characterised by distance or by intimacy. 'One thing you all need to understand,' she declared quietly, as much to herself and to the night as to him. 'I'll never go back.' At first he thought she meant to Dublin, to the college. Then she added, in a voice thickened by phlegm. 'I will *never* go back to the dust, and the breeze blocks, and the surveillance, and the plastic bags, and the ... *squalor.*'

A spasm shook her. She stepped out from the bin, plates at her knee, now addressing him directly. He watched a sauce tear meander toward the plate's edge. 'And even that maybe you could get used to. But do you know the worst of it? Do you, Oscar? No! How could you know, how could any of you? It's the certainty, the absolute, stubborn, unmoveable certainty that nothing, *nothing* is ever going to change. That nothing *can* ever change. And still you wait, and you ...' her fingers pinched the bridge of her nose as if she were fighting tears, but if she was, they were tears of anger '... you even *hope* (hope!), and so you queue up, and you wait, and you try to ingratiate yourself to the odious indifference of the little man with power, and you go through the thousand daily humiliations that waiting entails. And I know I'd still be there to this day if it wasn't for the little bit of pull my father had at that time.'

She tossed her mane of hair. 'I will *never* go back to it.' Then she clattered the plates onto the sideboard and faced him directly, jabbing the dusk with an index finger. 'I'd sooner top myself.'

He watched her turn to the low embers, a lovely silhouette. 'And I'll tell you something, my love, in case you're in any doubt. If it ever comes to it, I will.'

VI

Night falls, the fourth night of their escapade. Saturday night.

Oscar Finn's misgivings return with a vengeance. The stench is either more palpable or else his imagination has made it so. Nevertheless, he feels too weary to argue with her, too unsure of his ground. Her revelation has wrong-footed him. Also, the vehemence with which she has spoken. And not the vehemence, merely. There was something manic in her countenance when she recalled the refugee camp. Great hatred, little room. She said she'd sooner kill herself than go back to it. He doesn't doubt it.

But this stay, this sanctuary, is intolerable. The old man deserves his dignity. If he can't convince her on those grounds alone, it remains an incontrovertible fact that sooner or later, they'll be discovered. They need to move on. If he *is* to stay with her, that's the deal. He'll leave it until the morning to insist.

In bed, he lays a palm on the flat of her stomach; her t-shirt has ridden up to map her ribs, and her animal heat is driving the circuits of his body giddy. He's horribly tired, they both are. But he doesn't want to allow whatever their state is to harden into the awkwardness of platonic friendship. She lets the hand lie there. But then, as soon as he begins to stroke gentle circles with his thumb, she removes it. Not entirely, though. In fact, she moves his hand and pulls it over her breast! Outside of the t-shirt, however, and with her own hand in between it and any possibility of mischief.

All the same, he is able to interpret the gesture as a postponement of any decision on her part. And that is enough for Oscar Finn.

Sunday. An oyster sky. They've slept the sleep of the dead, both of them. They've woken to a sort of an understanding. Neither is quite sure which of them first articulated it, or even if it has been articulated.

He is to set off for Dublin. He has a proper rucksack in the flat, eighty litre; the one he took interrailing the previous summer. Eighty litres would fit enough clothes to tide both of them over. She scribbles out a list of what she wants him to dig out, a list of cosmetics and the like he shakes his head at in amusement. He may as well be raiding a pharmacy for all that he knows of women's toiletries. Across the breakfast table she slides him her key.

Once again she suggests Scotland, then maybe France. Though nowhere near the crazy brother, yeah? So he'll need his passport too, if he *is* to go along with her. Also, he'll need to swing by his folks. After all, it'll be the first time he's to spend a Christmas away from them, and his father isn't a well man. Maybe they'll offer a few bob; but he doesn't like to ask. That way he could pay off the petrol, say it was an oversight on his part. Otherwise they might stop the bike getting onto the Belfast ferry, who knows?

Will the folks be ok about him dropping out of college?

He shrugs. Probably not. He's eager to get going. 'Take this,' she says, handing him her Laser and scribbling the PIN on a slip of paper. 'There must be a good three hundred left in it. More, probably.'

He takes the card, doubtful. 'How come? I thought you said we couldn't use them ...'

She facepalms her forehead. 'Because, Mr Alpha Nerd, it'd be a good thing if their records were to show I'm still down in the Big Smoke!'

He smiles. 'You're better at this than I am.' And she is.

He makes for the tool shed, swinging the helmet like a pendulum. Against the frosty air he's recycled the pair of the old man's socks to use as makeshift gloves. Her call from the doorway arrests him. She has the farmer's cap pushed back on her head, irreverent and sexy as all hell. The dog is beside her, looking up, an allegory of fidelity. 'Hey mister! If you're a good boy, I'll let you pack my tartan gym skirt!'

'Nah,' he calls, 'it wouldn't suit me!'

Oscar Finn lays his ear against the flank of the bike and sloshes the tank. It is perhaps a third full, which will in all likelihood see him back to Dublin. But he doesn't know for certain it will. Nor does he know for certain what he'll do once he gets there. Use her Laser, obviously; but will he visit his home, ask them can he borrow a few hundred? Will he let them know he'll be gone for maybe months on end?

Will he talk the whole thing over with Nige, allow him to have a shot at dissuading him from this madcap road movie? He'll fill up his rucksack with her belongings, for sure. But how much, if any, of his own stuff will he push in on top of them? Is Scotland any more real than Narnia, or Hy Brasil?

He pulls on his helmet. All that can be decided on the hoof. Already he can envisage the bare hedgerows strobe-lighting the long ride home. The city must be a good three hours, plenty of time to weigh up and to mull over and to pursue the adventure as the cold air blows past him, as the tarmac river races beneath his feet.

What Oscar Finn doesn't know is that Gareth Hunt has had a second cerebral haemorrhage. It was a far more powerful rupture than the initial one. The diminishing series of bloody eruptions that followed was almost instantaneously fatal, and the body is even now being lifted with the callousness of habit from a hospital trolley, and is being laid out on a metal table to await the coroner's knife.

The very next time his foot touches the ground, the dream will be over.

HOME TRUTHS

It's the air that hits immediately you step through the door. The throat gags, just like the last time, and the first time. It refuses the tepid disinfected atmosphere on which floats a spoor of incontinence.

They must steam all the food in here.

Past the nurses' station, down the corridor already familiar. The marigold and lilac, the jaunty murals as if it's all a parody kindergarten. Past the shadow figures, their mouths agape.

The room at least has some pretence to normality. A private ward in a hospital, say. Her own books. Her photos. She has the television up loud, and is dozing in the armchair. You touch her shoulder. 'Nana.' Eyes flicker. They look up, fail to focus. You lift the remote from the tray, mute the gameshow. 'Come on, Nana. We'll get you out of here.'

Her eyes are still refusing to focus. Days, she drifts into some nebulous land where words have lost their value. Others, she's her old self. Her young self. 'Is it cold?' she asks. She's pulling a gargoyle face. 'Not so bad.' You're rummaging through the flatpack wardrobe, picking out a hat and the warmest shawl. 'It'll do you good to get a breath of air. Blow them oul cobwebs away.'

It had been a shock seeing her in the hospital ward. Not so much the rhubarb and custard bruising, the fledgling head, the one blooded eye, the ragged breath, the wheeze and drain of the tube at the corner of her mouth. It was how frail she'd grown, how tiny beneath the counterpane, as though the seven years in which you'd failed to see her had all at once caved in.

Loraine had phoned London, for the first time in months. So Nana must've gone wandering into the small hours. She'd been struck by a taxi. No, nothing critical. Bruising. A punctured lung. She'd had the call from St Vincent's at half five in the morning.

Loraine hadn't expected you to fly back to Ireland, but you had. You'd had to.

'Not a nursing home,' you'd told her, later. After the shock of the encounter; the rebuke of it. She'd chilled a bottle of Chablis in her fridge, a concession to your visit. Neither glass had been touched. 'Anything but a *home*, Lor.'

'You're not listening,' she said. 'The hospital won't let her go without a discharge plan. Blathnaid, they won't let her live in the house anymore, end of.'

'Not on her own, they won't.'

'Huh! So what are you suggesting? You'd move back, is it?'

You were twitching for a cigarette. Loraine had placed a saucer ashtray on the kitchen table, another concession. To buy time you lit up, drew in, tried out a grimace. 'If you saw the kip where I'm stopping these days ...'

She flinched upward, indignant. 'This is about Nana. With all respect, this is not about your youth slipping away!'

The venom stunned you both. 'That's not fair, Loraine.'

Something akin to remorse puckered her brow. 'And you'd be prepared to stay in?'

You shrugged: *whatever*.

'Because that's what it would mean, Blath. You'd need to be there twenty-four-seven. You couldn't just ... go out of a night.'

You exhaled a slow orchid upwards into her domestic interior. 'There's other options.'

'Oh?'

'Yeah. There's home help. There's ...' You sensed she was waiting for something to occur to you. You glanced toward the baby chair, the crate of coloured plastic, the crayoned Mammy under the fridge magnet, and you stabbed the cigarette into the saucer. 'I mean she seemed pretty lucid when I was in there.' You hoist a grin. 'So I tell her I must get home more, not just Christmas like. And Nan makes a joke out of it. She goes "you know where I live," then adds, "which is more than I do half the time!"'

A diluted smile. Maternity has made her immoveable. 'In fairness, you haven't *been* here. Half the time, she doesn't even know who she is anymore, let alone anyone else.' She'd donned her old expression of *I know more than either of you*. A drop in tone, as though she might be overheard. 'This was not the first time she was found wandering.'

And that was that. By the time you'd organised your stuff and moved back from London for the second time, Loraine had already lined up the nursing home.

There aren't many strollers out on the promenade. A bleary sun, a chill wind coming down off the head chasing litter in circles. Even under her tartan shawl, the Kashmir, Nana looks perished. You hurry the chair along in the direction of the coffee shop.

Once inside the warmth she shudders *brrrrrrr!* her eye quick as a bird's. It's too early to say how lucid she is, though. Nana has grown jokey with the years. 'Behave yourself now, Peggy!' the male nurse had called after her.

'What will I get you, Nan?' She scowls at the stranger who has asked. All her life she's had coffee, strong as a double espresso, even last thing before going to bed. 'My caffeine fix,' she'd call it. Coffee at night, and a bottle of stout before dinner. There was nothing Loraine could ever do or say to moderate that regime. Do they still let you have a bottle of stout, Nana?

You return with two filters. The shawl has slipped from her coat hanger shoulders, but some glow at least is returning under the cheekbones. 'Have you a cigarette?' she squints, not quite disclosing if she's recognised you. When you were still in your teens you used to have sneaky cigarettes together behind Loraine's back; Loraine, who was only four years older, but who'd grown up a full decade before you had. After the accident, she'd had to.

'You can't smoke in here, Nan.'

'Why not?'

You look around, for support. 'Coz it's the law!'

'Tsst! The *law* ...'

Loraine needed your signature. That, too, was the law. In order to secure power of attorney she'd have to get your consent, or at the very least you'd have to offer no objection during the time stipulated in her lawyer's letter. And you'd told her you'd be damned if you'd give her power of attorney over Nana's estate, as if she were already dead or crazy.

'What are you afraid of, Blath? You're afraid I'll sell off the house, is that it?' You were full sure she was on the point of adding *when we both know Nana will never live there again*. But she didn't. She always had the capacity to surprise, Loraine. Instead she said 'legally, I wouldn't be able to, even if I had a mind to. Which, by the way, I don't.'

'How do you figure that?'

'The government scheme doesn't allow it. We can't touch that house while it's being used to help pay for the care.'

'I don't see why you signed up to that bloody scheme. I declare to Christ I don't.'

'Because, my dear, we'd have to stump up a grand a week if we didn't. You got that sort of cash lying around, Blath? Because I don't.'

Cash. It was always a sore subject. Nan had run a frugal dress alterations business from the front room in order to keep the house after the granddad you'd never known had disappeared. In trilby, coat and scarf he'd gone down to the bookies one Saturday the same year you were born and had never returned. Loraine said you'd inherited his itchy feet. When the car crash had thrust two orphan grandkids upon her, Nana was already sixty.

'You could have talked it through with me first. You could have talked the whole thing through with me, before sticking her into that god-awful ... scarecrows' asylum.'

She blanched. 'You've some nerve! You think you can just swan back home after seven years like some ... prodigal ...' You watched her contained fury balk at the choice of noun. Bitch? *Opportunist*? She'd called you opportunist after she found out Nana had emptied her entire Post Office savings account to fund your acting course over in London. You'd asked for a ten thousand loan; she'd gifted a sum closer to thirty.

But who was the opportunist now, Loraine?

Nana is cupping her hands about the coffee as if it's a stovepipe. Her eyes are slanted and mischievous. Times like this you think you *could* live together in the house, make a go of it. Eleven different addresses in seven years, and you're sick to death of it. She's shaking her head slowly, as though she's overheard the idea. 'What, Nan?'

'Tsst,' she's pulling a face at your crew cut, 'you'll never get a husband that way, Louise.'

Louise, your mother. You scarcely remember her. But the communion photo of her might have been you. You touch your scalp, softly downed. 'I'm in no hurry to get married, Nan.'

'What age are you now?'

You're wrong-footed by the sharpness, both kinds of sharpness, and for a moment you forget. 'Thirty ... *two*?' you reply. Old enough that a lot of the best roles are slipping away.

'You look more,' she says. 'I don't know why you wear that monkey jacket when I got you that lovely tweed coat with the fox fur collar.'

'What coat, Nan?' But she's away into some argument she'd had with her daughter years before. The ancient paradox: as she's grown older her memories have grown younger. You touch her fingers, ice-cold chicken bones. You prise them from the coffee cup, rub them. 'I need you to be here with me, Nana. I need you to remember. Did Loraine have you fill out a bunch of forms?'

'I never cared for that Freddy,' she scowls. 'Too flashy by half.' Fred Nuzum. Your father. And perhaps she was right. It was a single car collision, the convertible wrapped around a telegraph pole late one Saturday night.

'Nana, please. It's me. It's Blath. Nana, did Loraine have you fill out a bunch of papers for the government?'

And it's hopeless. Hopeless.

Back outside, into the convalescent sunlight. 'I'll have that cigarette now,' she says. After you light it, she sucks greedily as an infant, the smoke forcing one eye closed. 'We'll get you back.' You push the chair to spare the battery; also because she's still uncertain with the joystick.

Back into the nappy smell. Once inside, she insists on manoeuvring the chair; a show of independence for the other inmates. It beeps intermittently, like a truck reversing. The male nurse is all smiles. 'Well, Peggy, did you have a nice walk?' And, as if behind your back, he signals with a wink a sneaky cigarette.

It comes to you like a sucker punch – she's happy here.

At the corner of the long corridor the chair halts, and you watch her hat tilt back. 'Don't be too hard on Loraine,' she calls. 'Sure she does her best.'

THE TAILOR'S SHEARS

For years, what most infuriated Emily Brooks was how entirely *supine* she'd been. Supine; it was such a Howard word. Were she to have those seven years again, were she even to have again the few weeks *after* he'd said to her 'look, Em, I've been meaning to tell you ...' she'd have given him what for! *I've been meaning to tell you* ... If there was a more spineless way of introducing bad news she'd dearly like to know what it was.

But that had been Howard all over. The path of least resistance. Of course, she was not *entirely* guiltless in that department. After all, theirs had scarcely been a match made in heaven. Howard Bale was never what anyone would have described as a catch. To give her her due, Dee had told her from the first that she could do better. As acutely as he lacked a chin Howard lacked determination, as if the one lack were the physical manifestation of the other. To have been left high and dry by so indecisive a figure was bad enough. Not to have taken him to task over it, not to have cried out '*you* will not do this to *me*, Howard', not to have landed at least one blow on that irresolute chin, that was what really jarred. At the very least, she might have taken up her scissors and made short shrift of his pinstripe suits.

True, nothing had ever been agreed between them, not explicitly. But *implicitly*, yes. After all, seven years had to count for something. Because they weren't just any seven years. These seven years had taken Emily Brooks from thirty two to thirty nine. *The* crucial term in any woman's biology, as even Howard's imperturbable myopia must have noticed. He was three years younger than she, but even had he been a full decade older, the laws of biology are far more forgiving where the male is concerned. Four years on, Howard was back in the London office, married to a mousy type he'd met through work, a father twice over by all accounts; and none of that would have mattered two hoots except that, in his bumbling, indecisive way, he'd caused her to miss the main chance. She'd woken from a seven year slumber, and when she'd looked in the mirror, a middle-aged woman with lizard skin about the eyes had looked back at her.

Spinster is a cruel word. A male word. As she examined the fissured puffiness about those eyes with a detachment that surprised her, Emily decided she would not endure the humiliation of placing herself back in the market. On the *Reduced to Clear* shelf, as she expressed it to her sister. Deirdre simply refused to see the lizard woman who looked out from the mirror. But it was a decision that Dee's vicarious indignation would find to be irrevocable. Any invitation that had the merest whiff of a double date about it was summarily declined, and after Emily turned forty, Dee stopped trying.

One other resolution was sworn as Emily stared down those lizard eyes, and it was this: never again, so long as she lived, would she be supine in the face of a coward's dismissal.

With Howard back in England, she'd retained possession of the apartment on Spencer Dock. It was a pyrrhic victory. The place was so undermined by negative equity it was all she could do not to be dragged under along with it. While

Howard had done whatever it was that he did in the IFSC to meet the mortgage payments, she'd dabbled in a dress alterations business. She now threw herself into alterations full time. It was never enough. So, as a stopgap, and with an unshakeable feeling of being violated, Emily took in a lodger.

The lodger was a Polish girl. Not what you'd call a livewire, and not *particularly* pretty, but young and, being young, in perpetual pursuit of a social life. There were ground rules. No boyfriends. No parties. Wash up to be done immediately after eating. And, by and large, Gosia abided by these ground rules. Her behaviour wasn't the problem. But now, every time Emily stepped out of the elevator, every time she approached down the long corridor her own front door, she experienced a feeling of trepidation that bordered on dread.

The relief she'd feel upon finding she had the flat to herself was comically out of proportion; and if that was true on a weekday it was trebly so on a Friday. While she'd been living on her own, during those nine short months that she'd had the luxury of having the apartment to herself, Emily thought nothing of opening a bottle of Pinot Grigio and curling up in front of a DVD, massaging any residual resentment at Howard Bale with the thought of what a wishy-washy *bore* he actually was. Now she felt she had to apologise to this twenty-something-year-old for the indignity of having no better option than to stay in on a Friday night. It was an intolerable situation. Unable to find a pretext for a row, in the end it was a moderate rebound in the housing market that allowed Emily to escape. Taking advantage of a debt write-off scheme, she sold up and moved in with her sister, Dee.

Dee had her own troubles. And perhaps that was just as well. For the next several years the dress alteration business that Emily ran from their duplex in Malahide was their chief source of income. As it expanded, on her good days Dee would help out. She had a fine eye for colour. Ironically, the line the unmarried sisters became best known for was in bridesmaids' dresses. But something else happened during this period. Something entirely unexpected. Emily Brooks began to write.

This had come about quite by chance when one of her regular customers, a busty busybody named Grace Delaney who ran the Rotary Club, inquired over her bifocals would she ever be good enough to look over a short story she was working on for the local writers' group that's all about this girl who's suffering from bipolar disorder, d'you follow, and seeing as your sister, well, you understand where I'm coming from, I hope you don't mind me asking ...

Grace Delaney was no listener. A talker, rather. It was at once apparent to Emily that any feedback should take the form of approval; and on foot of her several appreciative gurgles, Emily was invited to sit in on the next meeting. It was as if a light had come on inside her head. The group, made up almost exclusively of women of her own vintage, met every second Wednesday in the backroom of a local hotel. Grace Delaney was the *primum mobile*, though even her volubility deferred to an elderly lady named Phyllis when it came to critical post-mortems. Phyllis had had a chapbook of poetry published some years before. Of the two men who attended, one was a retired school principal whose contributions were of the *Sunday Miscellany* variety, the other a soft-spoken individual with John Lennon glasses who declared himself a feminist, who never risked any writings of his own, and who raised supercilious eyebrows over misplaced apostrophes.

From her first attempt, Emily gained a reputation as a dry wit. Her stories dealt with the tribulations of the single woman; in particular, of those who had entered their fourth (the feminist, with glasses directed toward the school principal, suggested this should read their *fifth*), decade. Women in their forties, at any rate. Not all had been dumped. Not all had particular grievances at their treatment at the hands of men. The most effective tales, though, the most witty, the best constructed and the ones that had most obviously exercised Emily Brooks' unexpectedly Gothic imagination, were revenge fantasies that leaned toward black comedy. The seamstress's shears had been brandished in more than one of them.

She began to wear long scarves. She touched round her lizard eyes with kohl. She invested in a trilby. In time for the Christmas party, a burlesque she read out about a self-declared feminist who was henpecked by his colossal wife had them all in stitches, all bar one whose thin smile and nods were at odds with his radish-coloured blush.

Emily was fifty when the first of these found its way into print. Within the year a second of them had been longlisted in a national competition. She began to rise up the pecking order. Next, a rejection slip from a well-known literary journal included a handwritten note offering guarded praise. Phyllis Deane encouraged her to put a collection together. Another two years went by before she had the bones of that collection, a third before she felt it was ready to go out. All twelve stories had been discussed and workshopped at considerable length; all had been tweaked or modified, shortened and sharpened. The only thing that none of the group seemed to agree with her on was the title that Emily Brooks chose for her collection. *Reduced to Clear.* Too pessimistic. Too dismissive. You do see it's intended to be ironic? Even so ...

Twenty years ago, she might have backed down; not anymore.

'Steel yourself,' Phyllis Deane had warned, quietly. 'I could wallpaper this room with the rejections I've had down the years.' Emily tried to. Still, it was hard not to take each *'we read your manuscript with interest, however on this occasion ...'* personally, as a commentary on her life as much as on her work. While she was safe within the group she could laugh away each disappointment; they'd all had their share of disappointments. When she was alone they troubled her. But they didn't infuriate. What infuriated were those editors who never got back, who allowed months of radio silence go by, who wouldn't even acknowledge, much less reply to a politely querying email. In the face of this deafness, several more years expired.

One evening Phyllis told her, strictly on the q.t., that Sadbh McHugh was now with Tolka Valley Press, and was soliciting strong female voices. Supported by Phyllis' commendation, she submitted the final story of the collection, 'The Tailor's Shears'. It was a dark fairytale about a dressmaking author 'with autumn-coloured hair' – the phrase was borrowed from a Phyllis Deane poem – who'd been pushed aside once too often. Everyone agreed it was her best. With dread, with giddiness, with fingers that were on the point of mutiny, Emily pressed *send*.

Before the week was out a brief email invited the complete manuscript. For the first time in an age, Emily dared to hope. She tried not to let on, though she did share her hope with Dee, who was back inside John of Gods and in need of a lift. Six weeks of intolerable anticipation followed. Then, on the eve of her fifty-ninth birthday, the email arrived. She was too nervous to click on it. She had to walk away from the computer. She pulled a bottle of Pinot Grigio from the fridge. She poured a full glass, drained it, squatted, breathed in and out as if she were about to give birth. Only then did she return to the desk.

The group was delighted for her. To be fair, even Madeleine, the resident bitch, appeared genuinely impressed. 'Do you have a firm date?' she narrowed her eyes.

'Not as yet.'

'Ah.'

'But it's slated for early next year.'

'Oh.' Her squint processed this, then opened. 'Well done you.'

'I hope now,' quipped Grace Delaney over her bifocals, 'you'll remember us when you're rich and famous.'

That had been four years ago. Four interminable years.

The first time the publication date got bumped no reason was given. The second time Sadbh McHugh apologised, but pointed out somewhat curtly that their Arts Council grant had been slashed, *again*. All their prospective authors were in the same boat. Several months later, in a circular, she announced that she was leaving Tolka Valley Press to take up a position in London. But not to worry, the new commissioning editor would be sure to honour all contracts. All *contracts*? Emily felt the floor of her gut plummet as she read and reread that circular. Did a series of emails constitute a *contract*? She was terrified to ask.

As the months became years, the group asked her less and less about the forthcoming collection. She began to hide behind a protective irony, and felt her standing diminish in proportion. A new editor had been appointed, a certain Colman Coyle, but no one seemed to know anything about the man. All that could be gleaned, electronically, was that he'd worked at one time on the *Carlow Nationalist*. Emily had sent him three emails to date, with a four month interval between each one. Every sentence she had agonised over, almost as much as she'd agonised over the dozen stories that made up *Reduced to Clear*. They were polite queries, warm, even witty. They showed all the deference of the weak. And Emily hated herself for writing them, almost as much as she hated this nonentity who never deigned to reply.

She reasoned and she rationalised. She invented excuses. Perhaps all her mails had gone directly to trash. So she sat, took out a block of Belvedere Bond and a fountain pen, and in her schoolgirl's hand she transcribed the third email. For seven weeks she watched for the postman. Nothing! At long last, one morning of ferocious heartbeats, she dialled the office of Tolka Valley Press. Even in the days when Sadbh McHugh worked there she'd never done this. She hated her telephone voice, which sounded as preposterously English as Howard's. So it was a relief when the phone rang out unanswered.

But she wasn't through, yet. After lunch, while Dee cleared the table, she pressed redial. To her amazement, not to say consternation, 'yes?' came a male voice.

Afterwards she wouldn't have been able to reproduce their conversation, neither what she had said, nor he. She did know that all through the phone call her heart was fluttering like a butterfly. She was dizzy and must have been pale, so intently was her sister watching her. 'Well?' Dee asked her, when at last Emily put the phone away from her ear and stared down at it.

'He'll see me.'

'Yes?'

'Tomorrow.'

That night she slept a deep, dreamless sleep. She woke refreshed. Perhaps that's how the condemned sleep on the eve of sentencing. She rose early, dressed carefully in front of the mirror. For the first time in a long time she met the lizard woman square in the eye. Now those eyes belonged to an old woman. Because that's what Emily Brooks was, at sixty three. For more than a decade she'd lived for one thing only, and that was to see her collection on a bookshelf in a shop. Every scrap of her had become invested in it. Now, that dream was to be taken from her. Because she no longer dared to hope. Even the trilby, which should have rejuvenated, lent her reflection a grotesque aspect. The wicker bag transformed her into something wicked out of a fairytale. She couldn't have said why, but before she left the flat, she lifted the tailor's shears from the worktop and dropped them into her bag.

Colman Coyle was seated to the rear of a cluttered desk, thumb weaving dextrously over a smartphone. He glanced up at the oddly-dressed woman who'd entered, raised two fingers of his left hand to suggest he'd be with her in as many ticks, then returned to the message. The air was acrid with old print and coffee. In a moment, Emily's gaze had taken in the state of disorder: the chimneystacks of yellowing papers; the ancient computer monitor on the floor; the unwashed mugs; the desiccated spider plant atop the metal filing cabinet.

Was she supposed to sit?

Emily decided she should. To stand until invited would be too servile by half. The only snag, there was a pile of books on the one free chair. 'Shall I ...?' she began, but the free hand waved impatiently. Alright, she thought, this was *not* the moment to be supine. Without setting down her bag she scooped an armful of books, and set about scouring the walls to find a free spot against which to lean them. Before she'd quite decided between the radiator and the far corner by the bin, the commissioning editor placed his phone face up on the desk, leaned back in his swivel chair, cleared his throat and, glancing twice at and instantly away from her, made a big show of blowing out. 'Ms Brook,' he said.

'Brooks.'

'Quite.'

Emily stood awkwardly, the books mutinous along her forearm.

'Look,' he began. 'Ms Brooks. It's ... I've, ahm, I've been meaning to tell you ...'

Twenty five years short circuited in that instant. She couldn't have said for certain where she was. Blindly, Emily's fingers reached inside the bag until they touched the tailor's shears as, one by one, the books tumbled onto the floor.

JUDGEMENT

It was the awarding of 'costs against' that finished the old man. That the case might finally be lost was a prospect he'd gradually come to accept, as he'd once come to accept that mother's illness was terminal. As the appeal drew near, Finley, the family lawyer, began to warn with increasing frequency and alarm; had advised again, on the very steps, to settle out of court, even though it would mean conceding the bloody point. My father was not the man for turning.

The case of 'Cafolla versus Grogan' began in the most trivial way imaginable. At the bottom of our drive stood a magnolia. This tree was mother's pride, transplanted the very month they'd moved into the place. Ever since the chemotherapy had meant she'd had to quit being an English teacher, she'd become devoted to the garden. Gardening, and also birdwatching; these, she'd say, were her consolations now, because although she continued to write occasional poetry, the muse seemed to operate increasingly at the whim of her noxious treatment.

At first the Grogans were sympathetic. The Grogans were builders, which is to say, Paddy Grogan was a builder, as his father had been. Indeed he'd built our place, all those years before, when there was nothing about but fields. I'd just turned two, so have no firsthand memories of how it was back then. I've seen the photos though, the rough field planted with improbably tiny shrubs, and my mum and dad with their improbably long hair. Good fences, they say, make good neighbours, and sure enough, no sooner had he laid the foundations of our house than Paddy Grogan had planted a row of leylandii on his side of the wire fence. The last point is not without its significance. The row of trees was on his land, not on ours. Also significant, that our property, which we held on a hundred year lease, lay to the northeast of that line of sombre monsters.

The years went by. The leylandii topped twenty foot, thirty. I entered secondary school. Then came mother's dark diagnosis. I say dark, because of a poem she penned after her treatment began. She'd wanted it to be her epitaph, but for once father put his foot down. Alright, just so you don't give my headstone any of your Cafolla photographs! *Malignant*, she titled the piece. I can still recite the punchline, which describes the dull ache abutting her ribcage: *'an eyeless tuber grubbing the dark earth/to give birth to what Lilith?'* I never really got poetry, still don't. Especially my mum's. To my ear it sounded like when she'd put on her telephone voice. I doubt my father got it either, anymore than he ever really understood his Irish wife. But that one has stayed with me down the years. Quitting her job was tough, but then my mother was one tough lady, and before long the acre upon which our house stood became not merely her world, but a living sculpture.

She'd been on chemo about a year when one day one of Grogan's trucks – they were forever going in and out of his place on weekends – took a few branches off the magnolia. Now, as I said, relations were still pretty amicable between the two families. They weren't unsympathetic people, just so long as you didn't cross them. Yes, there had been a spat about the tom that was continually fouling our beds and whose caterwauling on moonlit nights was the wail of a demonic infant. Several times, coming across a garland of feathers on the lawn, my mother had cursed the malicious beast. But he'd disappeared months since. I won't say that my dad was directly involved; I will say he'd throw me a sly wink on any occasion the subject had been broached by Maureen Grogan.

But the magnolia was another matter. The affair caught Paddy Grogan at a bad time. There was all that business with the Riverside Estate; the flooding and the backed up sewerage. And then, my father was never the most subtle of men, certainly not when it came to wording. As much as on her frail body, chemotherapy had wrought havoc on my mother's nerves, made her prone to mood swings and fits of temper as though to make up for the long hours of lethargy and listlessness. Usually she vented it on my hapless father. The morning she discovered the mutilated branches she was coldly furious: pure fecklessness had devastated the great plant whose arms, she'd always said, stood like candelabra each March. I seem to remember a poem in which she compared it precisely to a candelabrum in the hand of Persephone, thrust up from the gloomy underworld to herald her return. Why, then, she entrusted the letter to my inarticulate father is anyone's guess. I'm being unfair. I've no doubt he was articulate in Italian, or whatever dialect of Italian they speak around Palermo. After twenty years in Ireland he still spoke with a thick accent. But then, he was a computer programmer, and I guess interpersonal skills were not exactly at a premium in his workplace.

I never got to see the note he penned (and actually posted!) to our neighbour. Whatever it contained, it must've put the builder's nose right out of joint. A couple of weeks went by and then one morning a registered letter arrived from the firm of Bradley and McCoy Solicitors. There was some sort of a deposition; or a professional opinion; I was only fourteen at the time, and have never been entirely au fait with the legal shenanigans. In any case, an opinion was expressed, on National Road Authority paper, that the magnolia had become something of a hazard – both of our driveways gave onto a bend – and that it needed to be either removed or drastically cut back. The councillor who'd signed the letter was Grogan's brother-in-law. Needless to say mother was livid. Father too. Something in his Sicilian blood must have been roused by the blatant chicanery of the move.

His first instinct was to go to law. Two can play at that game, he said (he had the love of cliché and saying of the imperfect speaker). Mother prevailed. She'd have a word with Maureen Grogan first. They could take her tree after she was gone. Would it kill them to wait? After all, she'd remind her, when the Grogans were looking for planning permission to put in that extension with the picture window into their roof, and the Farrellys had objected, which side had they supported? 'But dear, we object was too high,' shrugged my father. 'Well it was too high! But we didn't object *outright*. That's the point I'm trying to make. If we had've objected *outright* with the Farrellys, there'd be no picture window now for them to look out of. That's the point, Fabrizio. It's as well to remind them.' If that tack didn't work, then we might try a countermeasure. In proportion as the leylandii had grown, so too had their shadows. By this time half of the garden was in perpetual shade, the lawn mossy and threadbare. 'Go you,' she instructed, 'and have a word with Fergal Finley. Tell him what the situation is. If they so much as touch my magnolia, I'll have them take down their precious leylandii, so I will. We have a law in this country called daylight saving.'

At this time, as said, the Riverside Estate was weighing heavily on Paddy Grogan's mind. To that extent, as my old man repeated with glee, we had him over a barrel; the last thing he wanted was another lawsuit on the books from another disgruntled plaintiff. The upshot was, without any recourse to Finley, not only was the magnolia left intact; the builder even agreed to have the leylandii trimmed. But he wasn't altogether the eejit. 'I don't mind doing it, Fabrizio, if it gives your missus a bit of pleasure. The only thing is, I think you'll agree it's only fair we go halves on the expense. Now, how does that suit you?' My dad held the other man's gaze, behind each of their eyes an entire ancestry of cunning. He too could be magnanimous. 'And we forget about magnolia?' 'That's what I'm saying to you. Have we a deal?' They had, they spat, and they shook on it.

It took two full days to trim that hedge. Special machinery had to be brought in; a cherry picker, two workers, a truck to take away the branches. A week later, the bill arrived. 'The guts of three grand, are you mad? Well the cheek of the man! He's charging us for the hire of his own machinery, look it Fabrizio!' Examining the invoice this was certainly the case; even the two workers (on overtime) were employees of Grogan & Son plc. 'You're not thinking of paying this, I hope.' 'Over my dead body,' declared my father. 'You think I'm born yesterday?' And that was when he was allowed follow his first instinct, to the law.

Fergal Finley had been the Regan family lawyer from time immemorial. Never mind the present house, it was Finley had signed the contracts on my maternal grandmother's house up in the village. It was Finley who'd drawn up, and seen executed, three generations of the

Regans' wills (a taxonomy of cancers had played havoc with my mother's side of the family tree). But he was semi-retired now, all his life had been a small-town lawyer, whereas Bradley and McCoy were city solicitors. 'Am I correct in saying there was no actual contract drawn up between you? The trees, d'you see, are entirely on his side of the boundary.' He and my father were pacing the bald lawn to our side of the mutilated hedge. 'No, is wrong. We shake on it.' 'Yes but Fabrizio, the point in law is that there is nothing in writing.' They paused at the magnolia by the gate as Finley sized up his client. 'Was there a witness, itself?' 'My son. He witnessed.' Under wild eyebrows the lawyer eyed me. I shrugged, as much as to say, what do you want, that's my old man for you! He'd have to find a tack more sensitive to Sicilian notions of honour.

The result, of course, was a foregone conclusion. It was round one to the Grogans. To be fair to Paddy, he'd tried to reason with us. 'Do yourselves a favour. It goes to court it'll end up costing you ten times as much. There's no one wins from these situations only the lawyers, and with your poor missus the way she is, well ...! Look, you can pay me back in instalments if you'd find that easier ...' He may as well have spat on Fabrizio Cafolla as add that last suggestion about paying in instalments. Perhaps that was why he said it; because as we were to find, that man had a vicious, vindictive streak in him. But then, as he was to find, where my father's sense of honour was concerned, reason could take a back seat.

Still, things might have blown over if fate hadn't intervened. A full year had passed since the affair of the damaged magnolia. Mother's condition had deteriorated, and that week she'd been admitted to Castlebar for observation. She was due back out on the Saturday. It was September, the month where promiscuous country roads have their hedges massacred, so that I wasn't surprised to overtake a leaf-eating tractor as I cycled home from school on the Thursday. But the council truck pulled up at the foot of our drive was another matter entirely. I immediately phoned my dad, but by the time his car pulled up, the damage was done. Mother's splendid magnolia was no more. I followed the train of dark Sicilian curses to the Grogans' front door. Now, it may well be that Paddy Grogan had forgotten all about the affair, as Maureen insisted. In all likelihood he had, for he had far bigger fish to fry. The downturn had left his business with a mass of debts and lawsuits. That's as may be, Mrs Grogan, the point was, from the moment he'd involved his brother-in-law, the councillor, he'd set in motion a process that had led to this crime. Yes, crime! And he must pay.

In proportion as mother's condition worsened, father became more intractable. Perhaps it was his way of feeling he was fighting her disease; perhaps his way of not thinking about it too closely. One way or another, the less time my mother was able to spend in her garden the more my father fought over every square inch and every legal scruple. I'm sure there's an irony in that, but if there is, for my money it's an admirable irony. Now, one unforeseen consequence of chopping twenty feet off the giant leylandii was that our house was now overlooked by the Grogans' box window. Worse, it overlooked the patio, which was south facing, and so was where mother liked to sit out on her good days. 'We should never have allowed them to build that monstrosity,' she sighed one weary morning. And whether that was the germ that infected my father, or whether it was a campaign over which he was already sitting in brood, from that day he began to show up at work less and less, and to be seen more and more in the offices of Fergal Finley and of Castlebar Town Council.

Mother died that November. It did nothing to dampen his agitation. If anything, it poured fuel on it. The kitchen table was taken over by plans and blueprints. A land surveyor was called in, and for several days our garden was host to all manner of tapes and tripods. Grogan looked on with sarcasm and derision. He'd fought his own losing battle with the banks, but he'd be damned if a crackpot Italian was about to get the better of him in his own backyard. And what it all came down to, in the end, was a matter of six inches. (I've endeavoured to be as accurate as I can in this, but Finley is an old man now, and from my father, of course, there can be no hope of accurate information). At the time of the proposed extension, unlike the Farrellys who had lodged their objections in the strongest terms, our family had objected only to the scale of the affair. The plans had been modified, the extension completed in record time. All that was old history. The Farrellys had sold up years since. If it was out of scale, the window had never been an issue between our families. But, meticulous measurements were now revealing that, all along, the bould Paddy Grogan had flouted the new plans by a matter of three inches. 'We have him!' cried my father, his fist pounding the table. Finley wasn't so sure, but they went to court on it.

It was thrown out. The judge, a woman, was not impressed. Fabrizio Cafolla was not impressed by the judge. By this time he was no longer an employee of Horizon Computing, and could devote all his energies to the niceties of the law. Finley he cajoled, bullied and begged, and between them they drew up an appeal. Justice Deirdre Brennan had ruled that the breach was trivial. That in itself was scandalous! No breach of regulation could be deemed trivial. There was a point of law to be ruled on. But then, added to that, my father had brought in a civil engineer, an expert on soil mechanics. He could demonstrate that, over the eleven years since the monstrous room had been added, there'd been a subsidence of a minimum of three inches. That meant that the original breach, the original flouting of the law, was a matter not of three but of *six* inches. Six inches, minimum! 'We will see that in this country there is justice!' cried my father. This time, it was not on the table that his defiant fist came down. This time, it was on the headstone of my mother's grave.

The appeal was dismissed, in even rounder terms. The old man still held out the hope that, in the matter of costs, the judge would be a Solomon. Surely he must understand that a point of principle was at stake. Finley shook his head, and the gravel voice of the law berated my father for wasting the court's time with such trivial nonsense. Costs, in their entirety, were awarded against, and Bradley and McCoy Solicitors did not come cheap.

The costs were ruinous. We would be forced to sell up. But that in itself wasn't the worst of it. Two days after the judgement, catching sight of Grogan's smug countenance peeping through the leylandii, my father seized up a garden shears. He made it two thirds the way across the lawn before a stroke felled him. It was the first in a series. These days he sits, hour after hour, in the nursing home, one side of his body stupefied with paralysis, his mouth depressed, his eye indignant. There are times, few enough, when I have succeeded in raising a spark in it. When I told him that the Grogans, too, had had to sell up, for instance. Or the time I told him that his father had died. Thanks to the small inheritance I would, after all, be in a position to do a law degree.

DUBLINER

The intermittent electric buzzer tore me abruptly out of a dream, a beautiful dream in which a huge, mythological bird had landed in my parents' garden. It was a vast creature, silver, heraldic, with a cry that was perfect and far beyond the threshold of hearing. I was reluctant to leave the vision, and so the dream at first tried to assimilate the insistent buzzing into its mutable logic. Surfaces bent and distorted so that the bird became no larger than a dodo, and the noise became an alarm call that rang from the direction of the gate. Now the bird was threatened and I was seized with panic. How might I protect it? The topography changed again, and we were indoors, the bird becoming a talking cat set in a glass cage, and now it was the cage itself that rang out. At the third mutation the surface of the dream shattered and I was thrust awake, my head throbbing from the wine I'd had earlier. Somewhere in the building a cistern was filling up.

I was dizzy, and it was an effort to accustom my eyes to the pulsating darkness. Moreover the floor of the bedsit was littered with clothes and discarded CD cases so it took me some time to negotiate a path through to the intercom. All the while the staccato electric buzzing detached itself and circled about the walls like a menacing insect, pricking and goading with its sense of urgency. My eyes half shut, I stubbed my toe as I reached the far wall and silently cursed to hell whoever had pulled me out of the dream of the bird.

'Who's there?'

'...'

'Who's there? Who is it?'

A squint over at the radio alarm told me that it was ten minutes short of three o'clock.

'Come on! Who is it?'

'Is Chantal there?'

'Jamil? Is that you?'

'Hello? Is Chantal up there?'

'Is that you, Jamil? Listen, she's not. She's not here.'

'Hello. It's just that ... I'm looking for Chantal.'

'Look at the time, for Christ's sake. I was asleep.'

'She's not up there?'

'I told you, she's not here. Jesus, Jamil, it's three o'clock in the morning.'

Furious, with a stale film over my tongue and an acute throbbing setting in behind my eyeballs, I groped my way back into bed and tossed onto one side. Although I knew it was hopeless I tried to recapture the huge bird in my mind's eye, but my consciousness remained too focused to allow me to drift back into sleep.

Now a few minutes have passed. Time drifts by with nothing but the night's indeterminate respiration mixing with my own breathing, and from faraway the sound of a can being kicked along. The darkness has grown translucent, filling the room with submarine buoyancy, so that I feel I am being lifted into a dark current of hours.

All at once my heart leaps. Outrageously, now, and again now, the buzzer erupts and interrupts in staccato bursts of raw electricity.

'FOR CHRIST'S SAKE!'

'I'll get it.'

Chantal has sat up in bed beside me, and in a single movement swings her feet onto the floor. Her hair is tousled, her eyes almost closed.

'It's that gobshite Jamil again. Leave it. Let him go to hell.'

But she is already on her feet and picking her way through the clothes and books towards the intercom. The neon light filtering in through the curtain paints a blue sheen on her skin where she stops so that I can imagine her sculpted in marble. I watch her as she begins to speak into the receiver and feel an absurd wave of jealousy that she stands naked while she talks to him.

'Jamil?'

I would have to strain in order to catch the static humming that continues for some minutes from the intercom, but the occasional electrical distortion casts a syllable out onto the night. These fragments of words confirm what I had in any case imagined; that he is agitated and pitiful; that he speaks to her in a peculiar patois that he knocked together out of French, Arabic and who knows what African tongue; that he has in no way changed or let go of the past. I permit the syllables that reach me to fall to the floor without making any attempt to decipher them, but instead nurture my bad humour and rub my eyes in deep circles into my sockets. Chantal's replies, as usual, are in English.

'Oh my god! Where was that?'

'Vvvvv ... vvvvv ... vvv.vvv ... vvvvvvvv'

'Ok. Listen, wait for me. I'll be right down. Do you hear me? Don't go anywhere, Jamil. I'm on my way down.'

She stands erect and looks at me, anticipating my displeasure.

'It's Jamil. He's been in some sort of a fight.'

'Oh.'

'I have to go down. Look, he might be hurt.'

I allow a thin veneer of indifference to disguise my irritation at this piece of news, and make no move to accompany her as she dresses.

Soon after I met Chantal we'd gone out, the three of us, to the music centre in Temple Bar. It was my first time there, not theirs. There is, I feel sure, an irony in that, although to tell the truth I can't remember if the venue had even existed the last time I'd lived at home. Ten years back I'd left Ireland to take up a job on the continent and now I was more a stranger here than they were. It was the old story, I suppose. In ten years the wanderlust they say our race is heir to had run its course. Like everyone else, I came back. Too many pints of Guinness drunk in the departure lounges of airports, and a vague nostalgia that I wanted to kill off before it had the chance to trick me with false or fabricated memories. In any event, such memories as I had retained were soon belied by the vista of cranes and multiplexes, of bars over-spilling with noise and suits and the hoarse bellowing of English stags.

From the very first I'd failed to warm to Jamil. He's a humourless type, perpetually foreign and ill at ease. Whatever the exact nature of the relationship he'd had with Chantal prior to their arrival here, it was immediately clear that, whereas she was anxious to move on, he was inherently hostile to anything that smacked of accommodation or change. He refuses to let go of his origins, and continues to speak to her in the fragmented patois that she only understands with difficulty and which serves to exclude all others. Nowadays I avoid him, but on that occasion I could scarcely have guessed how he'd be. Besides, I was alone here, my friends mostly married or moved on, and I was eager to fit into Chantal's world.

Sometime after the concert wound up we'd dropped into an all-night dive on Camden or Wexford Street to pick up a few singles of chips on our way back towards Rathmines. I remember I had misgivings the moment we entered the place. Bright, naked strip lighting, the air thick with frying and vinegar and, close by the door, an acrid puddle of fresh vomit. It must have been some time after the pubs had closed: bleary eyes and stifled yawns were scattered about the walls of the place waiting for their orders. You could sense these eyes variously looking at the three of us almost from the moment we walked in.

Even then, though I barely knew Jamil, I realised that walking into such a dump could only spell trouble. At one time it would have been a matter of accents, of Dublin 4 or 6 and the city centre flats, but now the mix was more complex, and no simple question of colour either – as someone once said, in Ireland we haven't had the time as yet to become full blown racists. Besides, none of Chantal's other friends ever seem to get into any kind of scrapes. But Jamil has a way that is not altogether ingenuous of standing out and looking perpetually restless, of fixing his eye in agitation on everyone and everything without distinction, of attracting the attention of anyone that is bent on making trouble. On Saturday night in that part of town there's never any shortage of those that are looking for trouble, and it came from the direction of the door just as I was paying for the order.

'Would you look at the darky pimp and his whoore.'

Jamil hadn't moved, but was staring at the eyeless red face in the hooded coat that had staggered against the first table, sending a tray of litter skirting across the floor. Chantal stepped towards me with forehead lowered. I glanced quickly past her to see how many of them there were, but could find no one inside or outside beyond the general public to whom the words seemed to have been addressed.

'I said, would you have a look at the daaarky pimp and his Jaysus whoore.'

Chantal touched my arm lightly in a gesture that said 'let's go quietly before there are fists thrown', but Jamil was still rigid, frozen, his back pressed to the wall and his eyes fixed on the figure of the drunk who had now flopped untidily into the chair by the door. The latter looked to be somewhere in his twenties, his face bloated and crimson, with eyebrows a thick black that might have been drawn on in charcoal. The hood of his coat left the sockets deep in shadow.

The entire chip shop had turned into a frieze, a tableau of glances or turned backs that were defined and held fast by the ugly challenge still hanging in the air.

'Come on, we're out of here.'

I touched Jamil's shoulder as I passed him, but he shrugged it away and refused even to look at me. So I put my arm around Chantal to steer her safely past the sprawling drunk. Just as we rounded him he leaned backwards and the hood fell clear of his head. A crew cut, tight to the scalp, and the tattoo of a dog at the side of the neck. But his eyes were unfocused and almost whimsical, at odds with the thick menace of his words. He raised his hand vaguely up, vaguely towards me.

'Are you right, boss? *An bhfuil an cailín leatsa?*'

I thought of stopping, but Chantal squeezed my forearm tightly and pulled me on towards the door. I hesitated again as the damp air of the night struck me, but she pulled me on with ever greater urgency.

'Leave it. He's a drunk. He's just a stupid drunk.'

'But what about ...?'

'Come on. Jamil will follow us. He'll be out in a moment.'

But he wasn't. We waited, concealed in a doorway about fifty yards up the street, but there was no sign of Jamil. After a couple of minutes I grew uneasy, released myself from Chantal's grip and made back through the drizzle towards the takeaway.

Through the misted window the scene looked almost exactly as I had left it. Jamil was set like a statue against the wall, his eyes fixed on the drunk who had now slumped over the table by the door. He seemed to be tense, coiled, waiting for the word or gesture that would release the trigger of his anger and set him upon the figure in the coat. But the man remained mute, slumped, his head buried in the crook of an elbow.

Then a mouth started laughing by the counter, a set of teeth and a gold earring in a leather jacket that had been finishing off a kebab. The gorgon's stare was immediately upon him, bulging whites of eyes that leapt out from the dark skin. The look was met, repudiated. A hand was pulled across the sniggering jaw. Jamil removed himself from the wall and let out a stream of foreign words that, for being unintelligible, sounded all the more challenging. Two other leather jackets stood up from a table, triangulating with the first. The jet of tribal words continued without a single pause for breath as Jamil made for the three of them. So rapidly did he move, so unexpectedly, that fists and boots were flying by the time I realised what was about to happen and jumped in to pull him away. Of course, by then it was too late. I lost half a pint of blood that night, and very nearly an eye.

The night condenses, lightens, slips away from me. Chantal has been gone for more than two hours now, and I don't expect her back before evening. She said she was going to take Jamil as far as Tallaght Hospital. Another scrap. Another dozen stitches. Whether he looked for it on this occasion or whether it wasn't his fault I neither know nor care. Whether they've begun seeing one another again, I also neither know nor care.

The February night has passed by, and a cold grey is breaking behind Rathmines clock tower. To the east, the arc of the bay will be turned to aluminium foil, whitened in occasional furrow by the approach of a dawn car ferry. The city will begin to wake, and soon the streets will be grid-locked with traffic. Somewhere towards the mountains, from a window in casualty, Chantal will watch the pale disc of a sun climb low in the metallic sky, antiseptic, the white phantom sun that barely serves to warm the air here.

Perhaps I'll stay. Perhaps I'll return to the continent. One way or another, I'll have cleared the ground of the first snares of false memory that I'd begun to fear. I'll be ten years older, abruptly, though wiser only in what I've turned my back on.

An age ago I went away, and while I was gone the whole city slipped slowly away from me, as slowly as the passing of years and seasons, of weeks and days, of hours, the passing of hours.

LOBSTERPOT

Mulligan pushed on his eyes with the heel of his palms and sifted, amidst the sparks and detonations, the shards from the night before. Lights. Voices. Grins. The electric rush of a DART. Svetlana Petrovna, tossing pinched breadcrumbs at his glass from across the table. The burn of a spliff. The wet towel that struggled underneath his jacket.

Hard to make it cohere. Any of it.

Another dry ebb of pain threatened his head. Eyes swaddled, he breathed in, breathed out. A hand tapped blindly for the coffee. Its clumsiness all but upset the contents over the keyboard. Just in time he righted the mug, saved the spill, raised it. But the mere thought of having to swallow brought on a dry retch.

He eased his lids into a squint. Office lights, forensically bright; one on the blink, wincing off and on. Even with eyes clamped he couldn't escape its insistent tinnitus. He sat up, swallowed dryness, then tried to focus again on the letter he'd found on his desk.

... we understand that high spirits often ...

Ah lads! He massaged the balls of his eyes, peered again around the unheated office. He was, for once, the first of them to have made it in.

Try again ... *that high spirits often lead* ... He blinked hard against the trembling sterile light. *Dear Mr Mulligan* ... But the type blurred as though he were looking through a cloud of fireflies. Only the masthead in bold print remained solid.

The Lobsterpot Seafood Emporium, Ely Place, Dublin 2.

Cartoon of a lobster in chef's hat. The sudden memory of wine it brought up was almost a belch. The wet towel crawling across his belly. Dún Laoghaire harbour's enormous claw about blackness reflecting boat lights, red and green.

He rubbed his eyes, prised each of them wide open between finger and thumb.

While we understand that high spirits often lead to high jinks ...

Mulligan panted, swallowed.

... *you'll understand that such behaviour as yours* ...

From the moment he'd woken to the clamour of a hangover a bare half hour ago, Mulligan had been vice-gripped by guilt. A conviction, unshakeable if unspecified, that he'd embarked on something disastrous the night before. There was nothing unusual in that. Indeterminate shame increasingly lurked like a hermit crab in the dregs of every binge. Feck sake, he'd be thirty come April. He was getting far too old for this aul' craic.

He'd rinsed an armpit mouth clammy with saliva; he'd splashed a bag-eyed reflection; he'd dressed hurriedly, almost carelessly. But it wasn't a day to risk carelessness.

He'd arrived in just before ten to an office as empty as the one they'd erupted from the previous evening. Christmas cards and decorations hung under the blinking fluorescence, unreal now as the rain-torn posters after a circus has decamped.

The door to the boss's office was mercifully shut. He'd slowed as he passed, held in his breath, but he'd heard nothing. *See you all in the morning, people, at not-so-early o'clock.* Dinner for fourteen at The Lobsterpot Seafood Emporium, no less. A free bar, till ten. Whatever else you might say about the boss with his interminable whims and figaries, you had to give him that. He wasn't the man to stint.

Of course, it's too bad I can't be with you all, have to wait on a damned Skype conference from the folks over in Boston, business eh what? What's it all for if a man daren't leave his own damned office for one single night, eh what? Wish to god I could be raising hell among you all, but you have a fine night, people, you've earned it, and I'll see you in the morning at not-so-early o'clock. Oh, meant to say, their Nuit St Georges '98 *is particularly salubrious, I can heartily recommend ...*

In his jovial absence there'd been high jinks about the table so impeccably set out. Hard to imagine, still less remember it now. Three hours (it must have been three hours) gone in the breadth of three minutes. A lot of clinking of glasses and impromptu speeches, a plethora of nudges and elbow prods and off-colour jokes. Laughter, raw and raucous, under the brittle indulgent smiles of the staff. How much of a tip had been laid on to keep them on board? The wine had flowed freely, needless to say not *Nuit St Georges '98.*

At one point, though, he must have tasted the tail end of a spliff. He must have! He recalled the jacketless street, the cold air, the orange traffic, the taste of burn on the tip of his tongue. One of McWilliams's roachless bastards, no doubt; McWilliams, his smoking confederate. Had the lovely Svetlana stepped outside with them? She'd been known to roll a joint herself, one memorable evening.

He did recall throwing a bread roll at the same Ms Petrovna that had skidded out under another table, *tut-tut-tut*. She'd started that lark, a pinched crumb that had plopped into his wineglass. At first he hadn't been sure it was she. A minute later a second, bigger, wetter, had caught him on the cheek. When he looked, she was waving a lobster claw as though the creature itself had thrown it.

... while we understand that high spirits often lead to high jinks ...

One other incident he did, definitively, remember; one other image. That was the challenge. McWilliams' upside-down grin, hovering over the fish tank like a malevolent moon. He'd been going down to, or coming back up from the toilets, negotiating the treacherously steep stairs to the basement. Svetlana Petrovna must have been behind it too. Why else would he have risen to the bait? Momentarily he imagined a seafloor, the lightless depths, the terror of the monster that had moved too far inside the trap. Was there a moment before it became too late to reverse out of that contraption?

The next memory was so vivid that his skin relived it. When all but the three of them had gone out amid whoops and confusions and deferential smiles, the sudden plunge of his hand and shirtsleeve into the tank. It had happened before he had the time to think himself out of it. Once out in the new element, the dribbling beast was hefty and spanner handed, cumbersome as an articulated gauntlet.

After that the memories lost all coherence, shivered by the hangover's hammering into vivid single fragments. The charge from the restaurant, coats bundled over arms. Then the quick towel (or was it a napkin?) and the slowly squirming wetness pressed against his shirt. The fumble at the ticket machine at Pearse Street station, coins spilled across the concrete. 'Grand Canal Dock, yeah?' And McWilliams' guffaw 'it has to be salt water, you gobshite!'

The mad DART ride itself was gone, all but their giggling stares at the perplexed smile of the pensioner who sat opposite. But he clearly did see again the great pincer of Dún Laoghaire; the boat lights scribbling under the tinkering of stays. He remembered the marble water with the graveyard smell, the planking of a woozy marina.

He remembered, too, crouching low with McWilliams and Svetlana Petrovna, coaxing the lobster's dazed inertia towards the saving precipice. It was she who, mocking their manhoods, had pulled the rubber bands from its claws.

Dear Mr Mulligan,

While we understand that. at this festive time of year, we all enjoy a good laugh, and while high spirits often lead to high jinks, you'll understand that such behaviour as yours as you left our emporium last night cannot be simply ignored or passed over in silence.

D4 Media is a valued customer, and we have no wish to take the matter further, always provided that you'll cover the cost of the theft, for unfortunately, high jinks or no, that is how the authorities would naturally view such an incident.

A simple reimbursement, then, along with a simple apology, and we'd be quite prepared to let the matter go at that.

We look forward to your timely response,

Yours etc

Sorcha Fitzwilliam, Ms

He stood up, too fast. Best do it now. On the spur. Certainly before the others arrived, any of them. Or before the boss's door opened. Christ, anything but that!

He pulled out his wallet with clumsy hand. It fell. Stooping, he collided head on with his hangover, had to pause and steady himself and wait for it to recede. Eyes still coping with the wall of pain, he groped for the fallen wallet, located it, and slowly recovered the upright. His mutinous fingers moved gingerly through the contents. Three tens. He hesitated, checked the clock, made a calculation. Thirty euro would surely cover the ...

The theft! he whispered viciously, fists clenching and unclenching. *For god's sake ...*

Would thirty cover it, though? Forty, at a pinch ... There was always the credit card.

Outside. Air fresh, breezy. But every footfall pounded his temples as hard as the pavement. God why do you do this, Mulligan? Thirty years of age this April. Thirty.

Briefly he smiled, thinking of the lobster. The derisory plop, after McWilliams had finally coaxed it over the edge with his toe, into the night water that filled the harbour, down to the lenient silt. Would it stay there, crouched and terrified? How would it know, in all that darkness, which way the mouth lay, and the open sea? And if it did, at last, get out what would it do the next time it encountered one of those coarse contraptions baited with whatever it was they put into them? Twenty to one it'd be caught again before the year was out and served up on a plate!

The Lobsterpot was setting up for lunch. It was still too early for customers. Best do it now, get it done with. In front of the aquarium's lethargic effervesce, a spaniel-haired waitress was scurrying back and forth until his hand at last detained her.

'Sorry, is there a ... Ms Fitzwilliam about?'

'Who?'

'The eh ... the maître d' that was on last night, at a guess?'

'Oh! She doesn't comes in till evening.'

Spanish? Had *she* been there last night, charging their glasses, enduring their raucous patronising? Circe's swine, arranged about a trough decked out in silver service. Mulligan's eyelids shut and, to steady his sea legs, he leaned back against the aquarium. 'Can you possibly get me the floor manager please?'

When he opened them again, a young lassie was standing before him. Pursed lips but cheeky eyes. Grey. Those grey eyes had surely witnessed their 'high jinks' of the previous night.

He opened his mouth but couldn't formulate a sentence. It was as if all words had left him. So he thrust the letter into her unsuspecting hands. All the basic details were there. He pulled out his wallet, fixed his gaze there, and with palsied fingers extracted the three tens.

But when he held them out, the grey eyes were alight with mockery. He looked at the letter, to where her nail polish tapped the childish logo: a lobster in a chef's hat, and in one hand, in one claw, a tiny, smoking spliff.

'I think, Mr Mulligan,' she spoke, not without consideration, 'that some of your workmates have been pulling your leg.'

THE LESSON

Perhaps you need to have been a teacher to understand this story. Not the mechanics of it. Not the shape of the conflict, either – the generations locked in the age-old power struggle. But the passions; the pressure cooker intensity of the passions.

I'd been teaching in Enda's for seven years. It's not a bad school – by which I mean, it's not a *particularly* bad school. There were classes you'd dread. Individuals you'd dread. Not just down from the council estates, either. More often than not it was the parents giving little Jason or Jacinta free rein that turned them into such pups.

Enda's is streamed. That's the first thing you need to know about it. Not officially, of course. But everyone in the staffroom knows it. The kids too, they're not stupid. Naturally, there's pass and honours. Not even the most bleeding-heart egalitarian can argue with that. But in a community school like Enda's, with five or six classes in every year, there's plenty of scope for sneaky streaming.

Here's another thing. Every class has its own personality. Once that becomes fixed, it's fixed for good.

But how that personality comes about, that's the point. It's no mere aggregate. Look back on your own schooldays. Certain individuals, certain cliques, are the collies amongst the sheep, driving the flock what way they will. You win those over, or you muzzle them. Because if you don't, they've the power to make life hell.

Up until fifth year I'd avoided Luke Palmer. I knew him by reputation. Knew of the wider family, too. His cousin had been some piece of work. A grade one lout, twice suspended. 'Known to the guards,' as the saying goes. Though funny enough, not much taller than Luke. They were neither of them what you'd call physically imposing. But then, you don't need muscles to be a bully. Just a surly single-mindedness. And then there was Catríona Palmer. Single mum, of course. A minute woman, ferret-eyed and ruthless. Butter wouldn't melt in little Luke's mouth, as far as she was concerned. If his name came up at every parent/teacher meeting, it was institutional vindictiveness. She actually used that phrase.

He looked the part, too. He had the same ferrety eyes as his mother. Lifeless, lank hair he'd a habit of pushing his fingers through. Oily pallid skin with eruptions of acne across either cheek, though I suppose no worse than many at that age. A hint of down on his upper lip like a memory of something shameful; something shameful he was inordinately proud of. I had his measure alright.

Perhaps you need to have been a teacher *not* to subscribe to the view that all children are essentially good. Some are little shits. That's all there is to it.

Tom Creegan had told me all about Luke Palmer. Creegan is as near to a friend as I had in Enda's. Not a friend in the extramural sense. We never hung round together after work. But he was the person I'd gravitate towards in the staffroom. He was the one with whom I'd exchange wry observations. And he was the only damn one out of all of them who didn't look at me as though I had two heads, afterwards.

Creegan is a quintessential English teacher. Impossible to imagine him in any other context. The dry irony. The preference for recherché words. The weary use of surnames. He even wears a sports jacket with elbows patched, for god's sake. Popular among the students. For playing such a recognisable type, I should imagine.

He'd been looking at *Huckleberry Finn* with the Transition Years. This was the year before my big run in with Mr Palmer. *Huck Finn* and *The Butcher Boy*. And a film, *The Outsiders*. Everyone was meant to put together some sort of a précis. Summary of the plot, that sort of thing. Now, when Creegan came into the staffroom immediately afterwards he was bristling. For five minutes he couldn't speak. Stood at the coffee machine, scarlet-faced and eyes like gobstoppers. What was it Palmer had done? He'd put up his hand, all innocent eyed. Which was something he never did unless it was *can I go to the toilet*.

'Well?'

'What's the story with *Nigger* Jim, sir? Is *Nigger* Jim meant to be a good guy? Are we supposed to like *Nigger* Jim, sir?' He wouldn't let it go. Just kept repeating the word. Any formulation he could think of. With just that emphasis, each time. And of course, Roche, the sidekick, sniggering away. Because what you have to understand, Enda's is a mixed bag, ethnically. In that TY class you had Desirée Ezenwa and Nelson Nwakali with the lazy eye.

But just try call Luke Palmer out on intonation. Outraged innocence.

So that's the sort of slippery customer I'd have to deal with. I wasn't exactly relishing the prospect.

We're halfway through the next academic year. After Christmas I'd be taking over a couple of maths classes from a teacher out on maternity. Enda's was that cash strapped that instead of taking on a sub, our principal has decided to divvy up her classes amongst existing staff. And being the least senior maths teacher, the badass maths streams would fall to my lot.

That in itself mightn't have led to the clash. But Enda's wasn't the only entity in financial straits at the time. Seven years before, the very year I'd signed the contract in Enda's, myself and Angela had taken out a mortgage. This was the era of the mad scramble to get on the housing ladder. Against Angela's conservative instincts, I'd argued for moving our tracker to a fixed rate. She was unconvinced, said the rate looked a bit steep. I drew up a table of projected repayments. 'Whatever,' she'd said.

Fast forward seven years. Ange is on a year's sabbatical. Unpaid sabbatical. In the run up to Christmas we get a letter – it turns out the fixed interest rate is variable after all. Repayments double, pretty much, at the same time as our income is halved. We go a month behind. Two. The only thing for it is to arrange a face-to-face with the bank manager. But I'm the one signed the bloody thing, so it's up to yours truly to sort it out. Needless to say, the meeting with the bank does not go well. I'm not giving this as an extenuating circumstance. A justification for what happened. I'm setting it down to round out the picture. To give both parties their full weight. Because every crisis is a collision of two distinct realities.

For the first two months of the new term, Palmer and his sidekick have been waging that sort of low-intensity warfare that's part and parcel of teaching the lower streams. The smirks, the whispering, the incessant white-noise of insolence. Every chair was dragged, every instruction misunderstood. By and large, you put up with it. Because there were some who were learning and who wanted to learn. If you didn't believe that, you wouldn't last long in this game.

What was it pushed me over the edge that Monday? A Monday like any other, to all intents and purposes. Overcast. Slow. The clock ineluctably advancing toward the hour I'd have to endure 5-D.

Things hadn't been good with Ange. Tight finances will do that. But that's not it, either. Some days you're just close to snapping. A little push, that's all it takes.

It wasn't even Palmer that had the class off kilter. Maybe that's what threw me. As I arrived, a textbook came skittering out the door. Maths book, the cover off. Property of one of the front row girls, Aoife Madden, mousy thing, big glasses, who's now scrambling shamefacedly to recover it.

'Who threw that book?'

Nothing. Silence. Butter wouldn't melt.

'Who? Threw? That? *Book*?' And I must've sounded like I meant business. Because Desirée Ezenwa stands up, flirtatious. 'It was me, *sir*.' That has me out of sorts. Because there's a look that Luke Palmer fires me, says *you thought it was me, didn't you?* And I have to look away.

Nothing much happens. Nothing that doesn't happen every other Monday of the year. Only today I'm in no mood for it. My heart is going. Insomnia, I imagine. The first time I turn from the whiteboard, he has his shoes up on the desk. Not for the first time I tell him to sit up properly. Not for the first time he does the bare minimum. Two minutes later he's at the same lark again. Shoes provocatively butterflying. I've had enough, I slap them off.

Now, that's a line crossed.

Everyone senses it. The air is charged.

I drawl, drolly 'you're not in some saloon there, cowboy.'

Guffaws.

He stands, sort of. If he stood straight, maybe I'd respect him. But he's craven. Underhand. He mutters something toward his sidekick, something I don't quite catch. Might have been 'fuck you, man', though later Roche swears blind what he said was 'funny man.' And there's the trademark snigger, the sly eyes. And before I know what's happened, I've lashed out. Open hand, right across the face.

There's a gasp. A collective intake of breath.

I look to my palm, wonder why it's smarting. He's bent double, left hand beneath the lank hair. Other hand fingering the table. And there, to my horror, I see it. Small as a jellybean between his shaking fingers. Plastic, prosthesis-coloured. Also a disc on a braided wire. He snatches it up, turns from me eyes bubble wrapped in hot tears. He shrinks from my touch as though it's loathsome. Then he's gone, loping, stumbling over bags.

Roche stares up at me, frog-mouth agape.

'Go on. Go after him.'

By the next period it's all over the school. I've my sixth years. And you could hear a pin drop.

Angela knows the bones of what's happened. The mechanics. The ignominy. I had to tell her. Sooner or later she was going to find out. When I'm home all day tomorrow. And the next day. But somehow, I've kept from her the heart of the matter.

I asked Tom Creegan 'did you know Luke Palmer had a hearing aid?' He was the only one who wasn't keeping an indiscreet distance.

'Why, did you *not*?' he countered, his open face altering the question to '*how* did you not?' And that is the question.

To grow up on the estates with a hearing aid, my god …

If the principal was outraged, she managed to conceal it. As yet, she said, she'd only been able to leave a voicemail on Catríona Palmer's phone. No telling what the reaction would be there.

I'd have to go home. There was no question about that. I'd have to consider myself suspended. 'Suspended on full pay, you understand.' Word must have got to her of the precariousness of our finances.

I watched her lips move. Nothing was registering. Or if it was, it was as though I were reading subtitles. All I could see was that miniature, flesh-coloured implant, lying on the classroom desk. I found her staring at me. 'We'll have to give it time,' she said.

'Give it time?'

'To blow over.'

I winced. Because, she hadn't got it. Creegan, I think, *did* get it. But Ange won't get it, of that I'm positive. Not ever. Neither will she forgive. You see, I'm not going back. Perhaps you need to be a teacher to understand. I can't go back – not there, not anywhere. The mortgage will simply have to wait.

RAIN-MONGREL

No one could say when he'd come in; when precisely he'd ensconced himself in the corner behind the cigarette machine. They became aware of him, vaguely, only after the last of the featured readers – hair matted, beard unkempt, an anorak torn and dirty as though much slept in.

There was to be a ten-minute break before the open mic. Loraine gravitated toward the table about which some of the PULSE crowd were clustered, the final featured poet back now in their number. She supposed it was a good thing to see them here. Mark maintained they were too much of a clique to show up unless to support one of their own.

'Is she any good?' Loraine had asked.

'Not my cup of tea.'

'So why invite her?'

'Precisely because, my dear, that crowd will only show up to hear one of their own.' He'd been trying for months to get into their zine. Loraine wasn't convinced, but then the spoken word was Mark's gig. Only the open mic part of the evening was her charge. She'd finally managed to coax a weary 'oh go on, then' out of Catríona Coffey, the gawky, provocatively-pregnant figure with hair part-shaved who edited the zine, when she felt the man's presence behind her. Perhaps it was the round of supercilious eyebrows that alerted her.

'I've a piece for you.' It was a low embittered voice, thickened with phlegm. It well befitted the weather-cudgelled face that met her when she turned. 'I'm sorry?' she smiled.

'I've a piece for you.' His head flinched in such a manner as to direct her gaze down toward a gaping pocket. When she shook her head, not quite following, his fingers, shaking and filthy, drew out a roll of scribbled papers. The flesh about the eyes was so pouched and battered that it gave the disquieting impression he was looking out at her from behind a mask. 'Do I know you?' she wondered, and she must have spoken it, because she heard him ask 'I dunno, do you?'

'Well,' she said, 'we'll see,' and then catching or imagining a round of smug exchanges at the table behind, 'yes,' she declared, 'why not! Is it long?'

'Couple of pages is all.'

'Great. We'll put you third up after the break ... *uhm*?' she prompted. He chose not to supply a name, merely nodded and retreated back behind the cigarette machine.

The audience had thinned so that there were few in the bar beyond an odd straggler and a scattering of open mic regulars. It annoyed Loraine that the *PULSE* crowd had departed the instant Catríona Coffey had recited her performance piece. She'd tried to fix a 'told-you-so' grimace on Mark, but he was busy busying himself with whatever it was Mark always found to busy himself with.

She consulted her list. 'Next up, we have ...' she began, and it was as though her nod in the direction of the cigarette machine had drawn the figure in the anorak from behind it.

He refused the microphone. He drew a hand once through his matted hair, looked at each of the few who'd stayed on, then turned his gaze directly to Loraine and, without consulting the pages, he began:

> have you walked the streets the inner city streets on any evening
> dirty like this one when the rain mongrel is down from the hills how
> she brushes her wet fell against all the stippled brick and concrete
> until the air is thick with moulting
> pavements wet and glistening neon stained
> traffic sluicing water over asphalt and gutters swollen
> with their dull monotony of swallowing
> even the river brown and bloated pushing through the legs
> the low arches the bearded river gods
> the back of the ha'penny bridge a cat arched
> and people have you seen people pushing
> pulsing over bridges huddled past up mary henry grafton
> hunched up white faces tilted forward ill with haste
> ill with
> or stuck like wet petals to the inside of sweating café windows
> and how the rain mongrel turns low and hunkers under her weight
> of hair with night coming in early from the east
> then
> choosing
> one anaemic face
> out of the pushing crowd
> how stepping out you shadow the impatient
> walk over echoing pavement the step-clack heel-clack
> her umbrella a broken blackbird's wing
> the footfall echoing longer as she pushes up through
> emptying streets away from taillights herding
> early homewards along the south quay toward the dark-lit park
> up instead
> up up beyond Parnell's obelisk and the dull rotunda

He stopped. 'Will I go on,' he said, no trace of a question, the eyes unflinching behind the puffy, pugilist's mask. Loraine looked to Mark. Even across the dim bar, his expression was as clear as a semaphore: it flashed 'who the hell is this clown?'

She swallowed coin tasting saliva, a hammering fisting her throat. Go on, she nodded.

two shadows
faint fainter
like secondhands
one darkens lightens then another revolves then
start again at the next lamppost
a slow swing at your feet and her shadows too
clock facing
she's heard
stop dead
no it's
it's the stocking sagged she teases over calf
and you catch her squinting softly squinting into the rain
she rises stamps twice and almost looks back
step out again
into tangible air fine-haired where the rain mongrel
has curled over the city and will not stir again now before light
up past mary's the black church stuck out in the road
an island splitting the stream of the road and
see
she crosses over
turns up into a street of little low houses
not trying to look like you're in a hurry
not trying to look
a street of huddled bungalows and at the corner
did you almost run afraid she might be already gone
and squinting through the drizzle not sure
not sure you saw which house for certain
but what you did hear was the click of the front door
clear as a shot

FUNERAL BLUES

She lay athwart the chair, one leg gangling over the arm, thumb stroking her phone. Wayne shook his head as he cantered through the room, trailing an intonation: *I wuzlike and he wuzlike and I wuzlike and he wuzlike and I wuzlike ...*

Not looking up from the screen, she exhaled *fuck-off-wayne.*

'Charming.'

He stuck his head inside the kitchen – no sign. 'That's charming.' He tried the bathroom, empty. He glanced into the main bedroom. It was as untidy as before. He retraced his steps, examined her sprawl from the doorway. 'Where's your mum?'

The girl shrugged. For a while he stared, his arm pressed against the door jamb. 'Yeah it was great, Siof, thanks for asking. Beaut of a day for a run. I managed to shave a minute off my personal best. Not bad, eh? What's that, Wayne, a minute you said? That's pretty damned impressive. I'm impressed ...' His monologue not raising a sigh or groan, he leaned toward her. 'Siofra? Your mother? Where?' A single vertical furrow marked her brow, and her braids flicked as though his persistence was a gadfly to be swatted away. 'Shopping?' she tried, eyes wide. 'Ah! Shopping. I see. Thanks, Siof. Hey I'd love to stick around to chat, but hey!' he slapped the jamb twice and made for the shower. Her eyes narrowed after him and she thrust up a middle finger. 'Oy,' he called, 'I saw that mate!'

He was towelling his hair, examining in the mirror the evidence it was thinning, when he heard the key grind the lock. A muffled exchange from the living room followed, then the rattle of keys on the kitchen counter. Barely five seconds passed before he heard Siofra yell 'laters!' and a judder reverberated through the entire flat. The door slammed after her.

Wayne stood out into the hallway, a towel about his waist. 'You're back, hey?'

'How was your run?'

'Good.' He approached the kitchen. 'Shaved about a minute off.'

'Oh yeah?' Jessica was on her hunkers, rearranging the fridge, examining sell-by dates. 'I, ahm ...'she peered at a jar, grimaced, replaced it. 'I ran into Bríd Ó Ceallaigh.'

'Not again?'

'She cornered me by frozen foods. I swear that woman's stalking me.'

'What she want this time?'

'Same old.' For the first time she looked up at him. 'She says Bronagh's been getting texts.'

He frowned. 'Kinda texts?'

'Texts. You know.' Concern darkened her. 'Abusive. Nasty.'

'Yeah?' An image of Bríd Ó Ceallaigh's dour mouth and tweed overcoat came to him. She must've been well into her forties when they'd had Bronagh. Only child, gawky, awkward as all hell. 'Did she say from Siofra?'

'God no. Siof can be a royal pain in the arse when she wants to be. But one thing Siofra doesn't have is a vicious streak.'

'Ok. So what'd she want then?'

'Just,' she stood, shut the fridge, blew out. 'Could Siofra not be a bit more friendly? In school, like.'

'Friendly. Right.'

'She won't let it go. She keeps asking me.'

'I don't get it. Why Siofra? It's not like ...' He shook his head. 'Look, Jess, I know she's your daughter and all ...'

'When they were young they used to get on.'

'For real? Somehow I don't see it.'

'Honest to god! They used do sleepovers all the time.'

'You never let on.' He thought back to the last parent/teacher meeting, Siofra throwing a sulk that Jess asked *him* to attend with her. 'First time I saw the Ó Ceallaighs I thought they were Bronagh's grandparents. So what did Ms Siofra Kavanagh have to say about sleeping over at the Ó Ceallaigh's place?'

'I'm talking when she was four or five, Wayne. I'll say one thing. You're grateful for any help you get when you're a single mum ...'

'Ah.' Wayne pulled a singlet, boxers and trackies from the clothes horse. 'Before my time, my dear.' He sniffed each item before pulling them on. 'So? You gonna talk to her?'

'I have talked to her.'

'Yeah? And?'

'But mum, she's such a dork.'

'She has a point.'

'Where does she get that? Dork. That sounds like something you'd say.'

'She doesn't get it from me, babes. Hey, she's on the phone, she switches to that gobbledygook they teach 'em in school any time I'm within earshot.'

'All the same, "dork"?'

'Probs *Home and Away*. Didn't she once say I was a *Home and Away* wannabe? Didn't you tell me that?'

Jessica Kavanagh didn't rise to the bait. 'It's Bronagh I feel sorry for.'

'Well, yeah. Can't be easy having the Widow Ó Ceallaigh for a mum, hey?'

'Look, Wayne.' He stopped, the singlet stretched halfway over his head. Something in her tone had him on his guard. 'Maybe you'd have a word with her?'

He whistled. 'You want me to have a word with Siofra.' He finished dressing and walked out of the room leaving the towel puddled on the floor. 'That's gonna happen.'

Three weeks later, the thunderbolt fell. All the Transition Years were asked to attend the service. They stood in groups of two or three outside the church, awaiting the arrival of the hearse. There was a subdued uneasiness about them, the unease solemnity brings out in those unaccustomed to it. All wore the maroon and grey uniform of Coláiste Mhantáin, but with none of the customary marks of rebellion – the untucked shirt, the missing tie. Occasionally, they shot furtive glances toward the TV crew keeping a respectful distance across the road, and at the cluster of photographers hovering about the gate.

Far fewer were the parents – after all it was a weekday, and not many would have known Bríd Ó Ceallaigh personally. Of course, it was tough on her, first the husband, now the child, *tsst* terrible, can you imagine finding her like that? Awful. Course she was always a bit of a loner, our Niamh says. All the same. You don't expect.

And then those cameras, would you look, could they not keep their distance this once? Oh, I'm sure they will. I saw the principal having a quiet word with them earlier on.

Siofra stood apart, as far as possible from the man in the sports jacket and chinos. Why the hell did he have to come? He wasn't even her stepdad. There he stood, flexing his biceps next to Miss Breathnach, the PE instructor, and trying to look all serious. It was mortifying. He was literally such a douchebag, how could her mum not see it? And now it was November and the landscape gardening was slack, he was always hanging around the flat, or showing off his body beautiful jogging the promenade. Gráinne Ní Dhuibhne had actually seen him.

Her thoughts were interrupted by the black cortege gliding glacially through the gates. There was a flutter of activity amongst the paparazzi, a purr of shutters. Yesterday, TG4 had interviewed Éimear Ní Bhroin, whose Irish could be relied on. *Cailín ciúin, nach raibh i dtrioblóid riamh.* Well, that much was true. Still it was a bit rich to see all the pious pusses on the bitches who'd given Bronagh such a relentless hard time. As if butter wouldn't melt ...

Wayne Bradley looked on as the door of the stretched limo was held open, and the figure in black veil and dress was unfolded out by two men in black armbands. The plumage of mourning. He'd lost sight of Siofra, who seemed determined to disown him. Couldn't blame the kid, really. At that age. He watched the Ó Ceallaigh woman hesitate, then shuck off a guiding hand as though its presence insulted her. But no. It was something else. She was reluctant to enter the arched doorway from which piped organ music was emanating. Too final a step, probably.

He saw her look through the clusters of schoolkids, who watched their feet or nodded gravely. An odd intuition had him already in motion as, finding what she'd been looking for, she made toward the lone girl by the birch. He was too distant to intervene, near enough to see all colour drain from Siofra's face. The woman – she was frail but animated by the energy of dignity – stood a bare six inches from the schoolgirl. 'You've a nerve coming here.' All was still. Absolute silence. What happened next was that Siofra guffawed, a nervous spasm. 'You *dare* laugh at me?' A laced hand was drawn back, terribly, magnificently, and would have struck her cheek had Wayne's hand not restrained it. 'Siofra, go to the car,' he said.

A sound distracted. The purr of rapid photography. 'Miss Breathnach,' he was already taking a step in the direction of the purr, 'would you take Siofra around to the carpark, please?' and assuming rather than seeing that his request had been complied with, he stretched out a palm toward the photographer, 'mate, you gotta stop that.'

'What's your problem?'

'I want you to wipe those pics, mate.'

'I don't think so.'

'Give me the camera, hey.'

The man shrugged, smirked toward an accomplice and, turning, was felled by a shot to the jaw that nobody saw coming, least of all Wayne Bradley. But now that the man was down he pulled the camera from him and with fingers that were clumsy with adrenaline he began to scroll back through the pictures, erasing them. He was so intent on the task that he failed to twig the flurry of activity amongst the remaining paparazzi.

'I just saw red is all, Jess. Before I knew it, my left hand struck out, *whump*, like it had a mind of its own.'

'You do know it'll be all over the tabloids in the morning?'

'That's the least of our worries, mate. He could slap a suit on me for common assault.'

'You think he will?'

'That's where my money is. I know these lowlifes. He gets so much as a loose tooth out of it, could turn out to be the most expensive punch I've ever thrown.'

'I'm not saying you did right,' she squeezed his forearm, 'but thanks.'

'Yeah?'

'For looking out for Siof.'

'Jesus, Jess, did you think I wouldn't look out for the kid?' Wayne poured himself a third glass of shiraz – Jess had scarcely touched hers. But he didn't raise it. 'I ever tell you about my time in the boarding school at Ballarat? Nah, didn't think so. We had a whole string of suicides in that school. Three of 'em. See at that age, death has a sort of glamour. You take the dorkiest kid, and suddenly everyone's all respectful. Admiring, almost. The padre tried to talk to us about it. Long story short, the last one to go was my cousin.' He drew a breath, sharp. 'The press were supposed to be respectful. To keep their distance, yeah? But this one lowlife kept pestering my aunt and uncle. Tried to get details, right there at the graveside. Where was he found? Who found him? Had they any old pictures? Wouldn't stop. There was a bit of a blue at that funeral and all.' He paused. 'Guess maybe that's why I flipped this time round.'

'Will you say that to her?'

'To Siofra?'

'Sure.'

'Say what?'

'About your cousin.'

He snorted, considered, and swirling the glass dismissively, took a swig of wine.

'Please, Wayne. I don't want her to ...' Jessica looked hard at his hairline as though searching for the word. 'You saw how quiet she was all evening.'

'She'd a pretty rough day.'

'I've seen it before, Wayne. She goes into herself.'

'You're worried, hey?' He laid his hand on hers, but she drew it away. 'You seriously think she'll listen to me?'

Jessica nodded, slowly.

'Doubt that, babes.'

'Her Prince Charming?'

'Yeah, right. Next thing, you'll tell me you're jealous.' All the same he rose, warmed by more than the wine, and made for Siofra's room. He hesitated to knock, instead placed his ear to the door. There was no sound.

'Siofra?' he tried. 'Siofra, ok to come in?'

Quietly, the door clicked open.

Scorched Earth

Months after, the smell persisted. The particular odour of ashes – bitter, caustic. It lay on the tongue, mingled into other tastes and smells: nettles and burdock, mud, a whiff of urine. The smell of rubbish that clings to human habitation long after it's been abandoned. There was a sweet oily undertone, as if diesel had been spilt, or cooking fat. It was there long after the white feathers of ash had been scattered to the four winds, and the remains pulled away.

Three days the police tape had kept the crime scene out of bounds. After school we'd watch the forensics teams go in and out, suited up like spacemen. There was much media interest – vans with satellite dishes and thick umbilical cables. Faces we knew from television talking into cameras under microphones like giant catkins. Interviews with our neighbours, the Gowans, with the Garda Commissioner, with the local TD. Never once asking the right question.

Which link, tracing back, is the first link in a chain?

When my father bought the site there'd been nothing here for miles round. Stone walls. Whitethorn hedges. Sheep looked on our comings and goings with ancient apathy. The old lane that ran up as far as the field was barely more than a twin set of wheel ruts, a spine of grass down the stony middle.

He'd laid out the chalk lines for the foundations. Mother lent a hand. I was too young to be of much help beyond keeping an eye on the baby. The lines they chalked out followed a plan he'd drawn up himself on squared paper with only the minimum oversight required for legal purposes. In those days the hardware business was doing well, and he could pull all sorts of favours from builders and suppliers. The following day, a JCB huge as a dinosaur began to claw out the earth.

We'd been living there about seven years when Pat Donlon, the farmer turned developer from whom we'd bought the plot, became town councillor. It's funny to look at the old photos. How mother coaxed a garden out of that rough field. Gort Breac we called it, for all the stones we pulled out of it over the months. I'm in several pictures with my baby sister, Ruth, raking grass into a wheelbarrow by beds of miniature shrubs, open fields stretching beyond. Seven years on, even as mother's nerves began to fail, the place was finally beginning to resemble a regular garden.

It was as I was finishing first year in the secondary school that the Travellers first appeared. On days it didn't rain I used wait for Ruth outside the deaf and dumb school, then we'd walk the mile out to the house, taking our time, pulling lush grass from the ditches for Gowan's horses, looking into the dusty hedgerows for nests or burrows. She was four years younger than I, Ruth. A quick kid, curious. But even before she was out of the cradle, the doctors had told mother she was profoundly deaf. *Profoundly.* That word always made me shiver. I imagined a deep, cold well in which she was irrevocably trapped.

It was Ruthie who first spotted the encampment. 'Look there, Briney,' she called in her muted consonants, her underwater vowels. Music heard through floorboards. 'What are those people doing there?'

With the building of the bypass the main road had become a back road. That was why it was safe for me to walk Ruth home. Besides, mother was no longer content to drive, not with the unpredictable way her nerves were. Only on the wettest days would I ring from the school for a lift. There was a lay-by where our laneway met the old main road; a strip of common land where, in the old days, an odd car might park, or a tractor dropping off bales of fodder for animals wintering out. An old chestnut stood vigil beside the gate at the bottom of the laneway. The previous summer I'd built a tree house out of timber from one of the skips behind the hardware business. We used lie there on long afternoons and play games, guessing the colour of the next car to pass.

It's hard, after so many years, to be precise about which came first; the slow collapse of father's business or mother's breakdown. Certainly, all that previous summer, we were not only allowed run wild; we were encouraged to. Suddenly, there was no work. Or if there was, it was patchy and unprofitable. When he wasn't pacing about the house, the majority of our dad's time was spent chasing old payments and bad debts, sending out invoice after invoice. To keep the company afloat he took out a second mortgage on the property, though the first was far from cleared. So we spent our days in the fresh air, my sister and I.

Ruth was a miniature tomboy, only happy in dungarees and wellies. I taught her everything the scouts had taught me: how to whittle pegs; how to soothe a nettle sting with a dock leaf; how to coax a fire out of straw and kindling. But nights were another matter. Home, we couldn't escape the charged atmosphere. The worries and recriminations. By the time I enrolled in secondary school I'd more than a passing familiarity with such terms as receivership; cashflow; section eleven bankruptcy. Also, a vocabulary of darker terms: anxiety, psychosis, panic attack.

There were two caravans. To begin with. They were linked to orange gas canisters, and a line of washing hammocked between them. An old mongrel collie, tethered to a breeze block, watched our approach with coat ruffled up about its neck. 'Come on,' I said, stiffening, making myself taller. I placed a hand at the back of Ruth's neck. Because she'd probably want to pet that dog, she was like that. 'Let's get on up to Mum.'

That evening, Dad was in a right humour. Ever since the bank had begun to send out letters, he'd been on edge. Usually he tried to hide it because mother had become so nervous. For days at a time the glooms would take her. That was her word for it, the glooms. Then, she'd sit in the kitchen, listless, her hair unwashed, sometimes spending the entire day in her dressing gown.

The minute she heard his car grind up outside, mother was at the door. He was too preoccupied with what the banks were threatening to listen to her concerns. So there were a couple of caravans, so what? They'd probably be gone in a couple of days. Probably looking for somewhere to stop over, is all. Nothing to worry about. Ok, ok. He'd get on to Pat Donlon the following morning. Yes, he'd drop in in person, would that do you? Jesus.

They didn't move on. Far from it. Instead, a third caravan was added. Then a Hiace van. None of the things occurred that you hear about. No washing was stolen from our back garden. No tools went missing from father's work shed. There was, though, a slow accumulation of rubbish – old washing machines and cookers with missing knobs and insides on show like metal entrails. Some days, mother would find the energy to go down and confront them. I was terrified for her, a frail woman going hammer and tongs at squaw-like women with oiled-back hair that could floor her with a single punch. There never seemed to be any men about the place. Or never during the day. At night, though, I could make out their silhouettes from my bedroom window moving about open campfires.

Donlon was worse than useless. Father's expression. 'D'you know what it is, he has the sergeant in his back pocket, he does. And d'you know what else I found out?' Mother watched with the smouldering resentment the weak have for the weak. 'It was the bold Pat Donlon signed the order to close the halting site out the old Galway Road. That's what has them here in the first place.' By this time I was in my Junior Cert year. The caravans had squatted at the bottom of our lane for sixteen months. Every attempt to coax or cajole, to bully or threaten had been ignored. 'Maybe if I was to talk to them in their sheltie, or whatever it is they call it.' The more he became powerless, the more he took refuge in a weary strain of sarcasm. It could've been worse. In school there were several whose parents had taken to the drink. One had driven into a lake one drunken night and had drowned. Accidental death was the official verdict. The whole school knew it had been no accident.

There was one hope that father clung to that helped him stay away from the drink. One of the big multinationals was slated to move into the area. It was more than a rumour, too. It had been announced by the IDA on the national news. Not only that, but the land that was sketched out for the new plant, and that only awaited planning permission, included our acre and a half. 'All we've to do,' he'd repeat, 'is hang on until such time as the land around here is rezoned. Then we'll clear up all our bloody debts.'

But hanging on was no easy matter. One evening he sat me down and explained the entire rigmarole. By this time he was a broken man. Pat Donlon's fingers were all over the planning office. It was he held the balance of the land out our way, and he could hold out for as long as was required to force us to foreclose. Sell the place off like damaged goods in a fire sale. We'd be ruined, but he'd make a bundle out of it.

Suddenly, the whole business with the Travellers had become clear to him. So long as they were squatting on public land at the entrance to our laneway, there was precious little chance of us finding a buyer. He had us over a barrel, whatever way you looked at it. 'And Da, d'you think *they're* in on it?' We were in my bedroom, sitting by the window where the dance of the campfire could be seen through the thorns of the hedge. There was no fear of Ruth overhearing us, and mother had checked herself into a hospital, to get herself back on an even keel. Or to get away from his watery sarcasm.

'Are they in on it? I don't know that. What I do know, not love nor money will make them bastards clear out. I wouldn't mind but there's that new site specially laid out for them where the old GAA grounds used be.'

'Suppose they weren't there, Da. What would happen then?'

'Then? Then we'd have some chance of fixing a decent price on this place. By private treaty. Pull the rug right out from under Cllr Donlon.' He squeezed my shoulder, winked. 'Your old man still has contacts in the property business, believe you me.'

Another month crawled by, one of the worst of our lives. Letters accumulated, warning letters in red ink. Every day the bank rang. I'd answer, say dad was not in. Payments were now eighteen months in arrears, and that on two mortgages, not one. The hardware business was boarded up, the business account frozen. One day, a buyer came out. For an hour my dad walked him around the place, showed him the cattle grid, the septic tank. Tried to dismiss the encampment as a joke; an entirely temporary affair. At the end of the hour the man made a derisory offer.

Does the rest of the story need to be told?

I was fourteen. Ruthie, eleven. For three years the atmosphere of the house had been as heavy as when thunderheads are building. I'd watched my mother decline into a bitter woman racked by the glooms. I'd watched my dad shuffle about unshaven in slippers, cracking quips that no one found funny. And I'd watched Ruth, watching on silently. What future for her, if we lost the house?

The talk in school that February was of the tinkers' wedding. These were supposed to be mad affairs altogether. One of my class, Dan Higgins, helped out an odd time in his father's pub. 'Will it be closed?' we asked. 'Closed to them, anyhow. Sure they'd have the place wrecked, soon as look at you.' Word was the Bridge Hotel they'd booked for the reception wouldn't be serving them alcohol either. Which meant they'd have to close the bar for everyone. Sure otherwise it'd be discrimination.

It got me thinking. February 20th was the day of the wedding. Now, I knew nothing at all about Traveller politics: their clans and their feuds. Who would attend a wedding, who'd be excluded. So the thing wasn't exactly premeditated. What I can say, I sat up all that evening by my bedroom window and I never once took my eyes off that gypsy encampment. That night, no campfire was lit. The Hiace was gone. By nine o'clock, the whole place had a deserted look about it.

The old collie hadn't been seen for months. For a while, a vicious mongrel with more than a dash of pitbull had tugged and slobbered at the end of its tether, causing us to steer wide arcs around it. But it had slipped its chain, and had been poisoned on McCabe's farm after savaging sheep. So my breath began to come in shallow pants; my heart, to thump like a mad thing. My throat tightened. Because I knew, with that dry certainty that comes at the instant before you take a dive, it would be now or never.

Our dad was out, up at the Gowans for one of those inconsequential meetings that was aimed at fast tracking the planning process. For far too long the councillor and his cronies had dragged their feet. There was talk of the multinational looking at other townlands. It couldn't have mattered less to me. All that mattered was that my father was out that night. He wouldn't stop me. He wouldn't catch me. And the bonus was, he'd have a cast iron alibi.

Ruth was another matter. As soon as I was out in the back yard, I looked up to see if her light was off. It wasn't. But that meant that she was lost in one of her books. She was a devil for the books, would read half the night if she wasn't caught.

It was dark now, the moon a sly grin low in the west. Ok. Ok. I breathed deeply. I must've had a clear head all the same, because I thought again about what I *wasn't* going to do. I wasn't going to use petrol or paraffin, or any other what they call accelerant. Too much chance they'd rake over the site in the morning to see if it was deliberate. But I was well used to setting fires using only twigs and straw; had taught Ruth the basics of it. A small fire, strategically placed. Particularly if I opened the valves on the gas canisters. Chances were the guards would blame their illegal campfires.

I selected the largest caravan. I pressed my nose to every single window. That's one of the few straws I still have to cling to. Behind the gauze curtains it was lifeless. And I took my time. Any car along the back road could be heard for a good country mile. I opened up the valve, set the bundle of twigs and straw beneath the join where the rubber tubing met the caravan. Ok. Ok. I struck a match, watched the tiny flame leap through the kindling. As it did, I heard a yelp behind that put the heart across me.

It was Ruth. She was staring at me, her arms extended. She was trying to speak, but seemed unable. 'Ruthie,' I whispered, desperate to get my body between her and the nascent flame. Desperate to get her away from the place. She was staring, mouth open. Eyes, disbelieving. I turned her, but she resisted. I could now hear the eager cackle of the flames. She twisted and writhed like a wild thing. Once, she even bit my arm. But foot by foot, I dragged her toward our laneway.

As we got there, there was a hiss, a sigh. Then a loud rush. The canister had caught. I saw the flame reflected in the puddles like a thousand eyes.

All that happened a long time ago. The best part of ten years.

I'd known nothing about an old man. A paralytic, somebody's grand uncle. When they went to their wedding, they'd left behind a nine-year-old to look after him. But the girl got restless, snuck off to see what was happening in town. Christ sake what sort of people, my father asked, would leave a nine-year-old in charge of an invalid?

The garda investigation was inconclusive. Officially, no crime had been committed. But a crime is no less a crime for that. Months on end I lived in dread of a summons, a letter, a peremptory knock at the door. It's a dread whose silt I taste to this day.

We lost the house and field. At the end of that year the bank repossessed it. We moved in over the warehouse. I was glad to see it go. I could barely stomach the odour of ashes, bitter and caustic, that seemed to cling to that cursed lay-by. The scorched, grey earth, the scarred oak tree. The flowers in yellowing plastic, the rain-teared cards and rosary beads.

Ten years.

And for every one of those years the shadow of the old paralytic has never left me alone. What I lost that night was my childhood. But more than that, far more, I lost Ruth. Never again did she trust me. Never again look up to me and follow me around, like my second self.

TIME TO MURDER AND CREATE

I see it all. I see it all, but who sees me?

You could say I run the show. Well sure, you nod. From a technical point of view. The lighting guy gets the cues wrong or goes AWOL, the actors perform on a dark set. But that's not what I mean. Any button pusher can follow cues. Even in an amateur affair like ours where everyone multitasks so that generally I double up as the sound guy, it's hardly rocket science. Of course, there *is* loading up the lighting rig. And that takes up an entire morning. And there's the gels and gobos. Checking the wattage. The temperature. Fixing the barn doors. Programming the control panel so it pretty much runs itself. Again, it doesn't exactly require a degree in engineering.

What it means in the run up to a show, and even more for the couple of weeks we're on the circuit, I don't get the jitters the rest of them get. Nor, I suppose, the vertiginous thrill. What I do get is time. Lots of time. Also perspective. The skewed perspective of the lighting box maybe – shadows more marked than uprights. But what you get to see from up here is the fly-on-the-wall stuff. The see-and-don't-be-seen stuff. The faces pulled behind backs. The stage kiss that was just that bit too long.

Take that one there – her with the tiny eyes and hairdo far too youthful? Aileen, the secretary. A tongue on her like caustic soda. And that guy with the comb-over in the sheepskin jacket? Looks harmless, yes? What if I was to tell you he'd do anything to see his brother taken down a peg? And trust me, I mean *anything*.

I'd been with Hurly Burly maybe a dozen seasons the year Alma Flynn walked in on an audition. Just like that, no introductions. Alma Flynn, who might've been fifteen, who might've been twenty five. In fact it was a couple of months since her Leaving Certificate. She told Bev straight out she'd only showed up for the auditions because her people hadn't the money to put her through drama school.

One thing about Hurly Burly, it takes the circuit pretty damned seriously. Readings for the circuit start in August, though we won't tour before the following February. That year, it was *A View from the Bridge*, Arthur Miller's classic, you know it? Tight piece, gutsy. Now, you're not going to attempt a play like that unless you've got Eddie Carbone in the bag, and Beatrice, and Katie. Most am dram groups could probably swing the first two. But getting someone to play a teenager just coming of age? I guess that's how come you don't see *A View from the Bridge* so much on the amateur stage.

It's a small group, Hurly Burly. A matriarchy, too, to the extent that the only one who ever did or ever would direct was Bev Gardner. Bev's American. Usually, we stuck to three or four handers. Five actors max, with maybe a couple of walk-ons. So this play was already going to be a challenge. In Philip Rattigan, Bev had her lead – he'd won a hatful of best actors down the years and besides, Rattigan has a swarthy look. Could pass for Italian, and he can nail a Brooklyn accent. And then, like every am dram group in the history of am dram, we'd no shortage of contenders to play Beatrice Carbone. Generally it would've gone to Lisa Corrigan, Rattigan's other half. But she'd announced at the AGM she was six weeks gone, and she'd be showing come February. She'd be happy to manage backstage. As for the other ladies vying for the part, it was going to come down to chemistry, pure and simple. What worked on stage.

And Catherine, the niece? As it happened, Lisa Corrigan had a niece. And that niece had picked up a couple of adjudicator awards the previous year for her portrayal of Girleen in *The Lonesome West*. She was a spry thing, elvish. Saoirse Corrigan had only recently turned sixteen, so it was in part to act as chaperone that her Aunt Lisa suggested managing backstage. They could share a room on any stopover. So the auditions that night were basically to select a Beatrice to play opposite Rattigan's Eddie Carbone. That and to try to shoehorn the remainder of the membership into the available parts. If they could bury their animosity, the Donlon twins could make a passable Marco and Rodolpho. But as for Alfieri the lawyer/narrator, PJ Kelleher's accent was so bad the joke was Bev would have to rename the character Alf O'Leary.

Auditions were just about to resume after coffee break when into the hall breezed Alma Flynn, all four foot ten and spiky hair and faded denims. Now, it's not my part to talk about the politics of the am dram group. I can't say what code of ties and loyalties is supposed to operate. What I can say, down the years Bev Gardner never shied away from displaying her ruthless streak. Bev was all about making the finals in Athlone, and making the finals in Athlone is what Hurly Burly should be about. If that meant drafting in a new face from outside the group so be it. That was Bev's ethic, part of her American DNA.

The long and the short of it, Alma got the part. And seeing her niece displaced, Lisa Corrigan was no longer available as stage manager. To have been a fly-on-the-wall when she discussed the upcoming tour with her swarthy other half, now that would've been something. For she must have noticed, no more than myself and everyone else, that when it came to rehearsals, any time they weren't actually blocking out a scene or doing a line call, there was an awkward, you might even say an *adolescent* reserve on the part of Eddie Carbone toward his juvenile charge. What made it doubly curious was that Alma had a humour quirky as her hair, and she was forever engaging in easy banter with the Donlon twins. Also with June Mahoney, who'd unexpectedly been given the nod ahead of Liz Keane to play Beatrice Carbone – on foot of which it transpired that Liz's husband's van, almost twice the capacity of mine, was no longer at the disposal of the group during February-March.

Rivalry and envy – they're no strangers to the stage. Jealousy, too. You might even say they're what give certain performances their bite. Something is going on onstage beneath the level of the play, and the audience senses it. The time we toured *The Lonesome West*, the Donlon twins were barely talking to one another – there'd been some balls-up over their mother's will, with the result it was stuck in probate. It lent an edge to the play's sibling rivalry beyond anything Bev Gardner could have wished for, and if it wasn't for the cockeyed adjudication we got down in Carnew, that edginess would surely have carried us to Athlone.

Something about what I was witnessing was of a different order.

When was it I had the first foreboding?

There was one night in November, a wild night, rain driven fitfully against the windows of the hall. We were packing my van. I was there not because we were having a look at the lighting plot – techies and crew were not required at run-of-the-mill rehearsals. There was a bit of heavy lifting – retrieving the blacks and costume crates out of the attic – so Bev asked me to come down. With Liz Keane's husband's van no longer available, we had to see how much mine could fit on top of the lights.

Joe Donlon was the younger of the Donlon twins by a couple of hours, but those hours might just as well have been years. They're fraternal twins, not identical. Joe's chubbier, but if he is, he's also jollier. Always ready with the quick quip, and one usually bordering on the louche or inappropriate. People instinctively liked Joe. Not that they didn't like Donal in their way, it's just that Donal was that bit drier. I think that was the nub of why he resented the way the mother's will had divided the estate. Families never bear too much looking into. Of course it was Donal, he of the comb-over and sheepskin jacket, who I could rely on to help clear out the attic, while Joe looked on and fired his smart-arsed remarks. Alma Flynn was willing and able, all four foot ten of her, and surprisingly robust when it came to carrying whatever Joe piled onto her head. It was all innocent fun, banter, standard horseplay. But Donal Donlon was not enjoying it. In fact he was rigid with envy. That much you could sense, the way you sense an electric field. Was Joe oblivious? I don't think so.

Then, when I was leaving, or more correctly, when I'd already left and was returning briefly for a monkey wrench I'd left backstage, I overheard an altercation. Not Donal Donlon. Philip Rattigan. I caught sight of his open palm pushing Joe hard in the chest – I assume they'd both stepped outside for a fag. There was a guffaw, then 'I see you try that on again, or anything like it, I'll fucking kill you myself.' It was a hiss. A whisper through clenched teeth. Was Rattigan messing? I didn't stick round to find out. I didn't want either of them to think I was snooping.

Ok, it's not exactly forensic evidence. All the same I could see Alma Flynn's presence was setting the men like game cocks one against another. Not her fault, but there you are. But that's a long way from saying I knew what it was going to lead to.

I was pretty much out of the loop until the tech rehearsal in January. As I say, the lighting guy isn't required at most rehearsals. And it was during that endless day that I was witness to how far things had moved on. From my perch in the lighting box I had the time and the opportunity to observe. Now, it's fairly normal during a play run for people to live in one another's pockets. Sometimes there's a bit of spill over from the story the playwright wrote. So I wasn't entirely surprised to see the rapport, the ne'er-see-one-without-the-other, between Alma and Philip Rattigan. She was hungry for the circuit, she'd never been on it – remember, she was still only seventeen. And he had the glamour of the veteran.

How far had things gone? I can't say. Donlon was fidgety as all hell. Joe, I mean. It all seemed to pass Donal by. And remember Aileen, her with the tiny eyes and hairdo far too youthful? She was making it her business to never leave the two leads out of sight if she could help it. She'd always had a thing for Philip Rattigan, that much was well known. And with so much discontent among the other members of Hurly Burly, Aileen was now stage manager. I didn't see anything that day that would hold up in court. But body language tells its own story. And banter. That stage kiss that goes on just a bit too long? That's what I'm talking about.

The run of three nights in the town hall prior to the circuit passed without any major balls-ups. A few cues missed, a prop or two misplaced. But against that there was an electric charge that pulsed under the boards pretty much from the minute Rodolpho encroached on Eddie Carbone's territory. You really felt these two guys could have a go at one another. Bev sensed it, and Bev loved it.

I'd never seen her so excited about the prospects of finally making Athlone.

But it was a powder keg. All it needed was a spark to set it off.

On the night before we were to head off on the circuit, Lisa Corrigan received an anonymous note. By this time she was seven months gone. The note was short and brutal. Whatever the truth behind it, it was a dirty underhand blow. It could've caused all sorts of complications with the pregnancy. I don't know what went down that night between Lisa and Philip Rattigan. What I do know, that first night down in Gorey, he looked like a man who hadn't slept a wink. And I have more than an idea it was Joe Donlon he suspected of writing that note, though to my mind it was more in the style of our piggy-eyed secretary. But all that gave his performance a desperate jumpiness. Long and the short of it, we came away with best play and best actor. And a nomination for Alma Flynn, on her very first outing.

There are any number of accidents that might befall a touring company, unused to the small-town stage with its precise hazards. A light might crash down from the rig, its safety tether improperly tied; or a ladder might be insecurely balanced at the edge of a rostrum as the set is being dressed; or a trapdoor left open. You don't brace a flat, it can topple at the slightest disturbance – eight foot by four, with who knows what screwed into it. It's not a fall you'd want to be on the receiving end of.

And then there's the props. Ever considered how easy it would be for someone to tamper with them as they lie innocuously on the props table? I don't even mean the *Murder, She Wrote* kind of stuff – the unbated sword, the dagger with the retracting blade that fails to retract; the revolver that's supposed to be loaded with blanks. Or the cold tea in the brandy decanter laced with arsenic. Or say I was in on the act – the lights go out, and when they come up again, there's an actual body centre stage. All very well in a TV drama, or in an Agatha Christie you might actually see on the circuit.

But ... *a peanut*? Has a peanut ever been used as a murder weapon?

Yet that night in Goresbridge – it was our fifth night on the circuit – no sooner had Eddie Carbone forced the infamous kiss on Rodolpho than the latter went into spasms. Anaphylactic shock. That's the simple, medical fact. At first the audience thought it was part of the production, something you might see in a Jacobean revenge play. But then I brought the lights up, and someone in-house was quick to close the curtains. *Rhubarb, rhubarb, rhubarb, pssh, pssh, pssh*. By the time I was down from the lighting box and onto the stage, Joe Donlon was rigid, bug-eyed, purple and gasping like a landed fish. His brother had jabbed some sort of hypodermic into him, but it didn't appear to be having much effect.

Ok, he didn't die. During the ambulance ride the paramedics managed to control the spasms and open his throat. But it was a close run thing.

Philip Rattigan denied he'd been next or near a peanut that day. Alma, Bev and PJ Kelleher had dined with him prior to the show, so there was no evidence to the contrary. He did mention an odd taste off the bottle of Jameson that Eddie Carbone necks just prior to that kiss – could it really have been smeared with peanut oil? And by whom, for god's sake? Which of us, bar Donal, knew that Joe had a dangerous peanut allergy? Ok, he'd thrown a wobbler that time in the Chinese after the AGM – but that was seven years ago, and besides, sesame oil had been the culprit then.

Could it all have been an unhappy accident? After all the hullabaloo the Jameson bottle went missing. But then we only went to look for it the following day, after Joe had been given the all-clear and the scare was over. The Gardaí hadn't been called. Why would they have been? Strong allergic reactions occur every day of the week.

Goresbridge was a write-off, and we pulled out of Skerries, which was to have been the following night. But hats off to Joe. If he suspected someone had had a go at him – and who knows but it might even have been his older brother – he wasn't the one to show it, or to let it get to him. In fact, if anything, the final two shows had even more edge than any that had gone down before. And heel of the hunt, we've made Athlone.

It's an hour to curtain. And even I am starting to get the jitters.

There have been a few minor changes. Lisa Corrigan has come down, basketball bump or no, to help out backstage. And there's no love lost between herself and Aileen of the piggy eyes and too-youthful hairdo. But if Lisa was worried about Alma Flynn, she needn't have been. When Alma learned about that little anonymous note she was horrified. It poured cold water on the whole offstage love-in between herself and Rattigan. These days she's all about Joe, who came out of the peanut fiasco with colours flying. Making a joke of the whole thing. Letting on to have an asthmatic attack any time the word nut is so much as mentioned. Rattigan can't stand to be in the same room as him. And for Alma, that's hurtful. She really just wants us all to be one big happy family.

I see it all. I see it all from my hideaway. I saw who it was placed that bottle of Jameson on the props table, and I've a fair idea of who made that same bottle disappear. But I've kept it to myself. It might surprise you to hear who it was.

I've never seen Bev Gardner so fired up. Fiddling, fussing. An eye to every detail. And I honestly think we've a shot, this time. If we can keep the company from killing one another, that is.

ZITHER MUSIC

We'd been to the Gate to watch Barry McGovern do his Beckett thing. A character whose proportions might've been dreamed up by Alberto Giacometti. McGovern's, not Beckett's. Then across to Conway's for pints. This is before they shut the place down. Before the smoking ban kicked in and everything became euro.

Ruthie was giving it 'what was the story with that story, anyhow?' Throaty Monaghan accent, like everything is a big joke.

'Which story?'

'That malarkey about being attacked by a family of weasels.'

'A tribe of stoats,' sighed Johnny D, lenses flashing in my direction.

'Are they not the same thing?'

'Fucked if I know,' I say.

'I don't get it, but. How can you guys say he's *funny*?'

'*Funny*? He's fucking hilarious!' And *that* is Johnny all over. Whatever Ruthie said, John D was bound to take the opposite tack. Only this time he wasn't stirring it just for devilment. I know him on this one. But now Ruthie's looking to me like I'm meant to adjudicate between them. Which would be grand, except for on the one hand I'm with Johnny, I always found old Sam not exactly hilarious, but funny. Droll, you know? Deadpan. And on the other hand, I have the serious hots for Ruth McArdle. I never let on. As if I needed to. She's one smart cookie.

So I'm 'well he's not exactly Billy fucking Connolly.' Which is about the worst thing I could've said. Because now I'm caught between Johnny D's antenna eyebrows twittering *oh yeah?* and Ruth McArdle's not-one-bit-impressed puss, which looks like it's had about a dozen injections of Botox it's that immobile.

Maybe a change of tack? 'I'm not sure he got it either. Left off writing it by all accounts. Notes from an unfinished work.'

'Abandoned would be the *mot juste*, Maguire.'

'Whatever. My point being maybe ole Sam got bored of his stoats.'

But Ruthie's having none of it – my sitting on the fence. 'So is he?' Pause. '*Hilarious?*'

Now here's the crux. Johnny can be really fucking annoying. When we were over in the Gate, he'd been doing that thing of the extra-loud guffaw, showing off how he got the gag and all. And Ruthie's unimpressed look is telling me that if I take his side of the argument it'll smack to her of betrayal. But then I don't want to betray Beckett, which I realise sounds Looney Tunes. The way I'm caught in their pincer stares I'm not going to be allowed let it drop, either. It's what you might call a nice dilemma. Bar everything else it's Johnny's round. And he has no intention of moving from the table before the matter is put to bed.

'Is he *hilarious*?' I consider the flier from the Gate. 'Can I phone a friend?'

No one budges. The pincers tighten.

Another tack, running downwind. I iron the flier flat on the wet table. That black and white photo you've seen a dozen times. 'Ever strike either of you how heraldic Beckett is? Like a griffin out of a bestiary. Or a seagull, say, to Yeats' heron. Which would make Jimmy Joyce what ... an owl maybe?'

No one bites. Now, a cartoon angel is whispering into my right ear how if I play it wrong I'll be stuck all night in the supercilious company of Johnathon Dowling Esq. Reason is screaming to hand Ruth McArdle her little victory. Hilarious is not the *mot juste* where Beckett is concerned. But, not for the first time, my left ear is assailed by the seductive whisper of the Imp of the Perverse. 'Nah,' I say, slapping the empty glass gavel-like on the wet flier and disarticulating Beckett's forehead. 'He's pretty damn funny. Dark. But yeah. Funny.' With the result that all through the next round Ruth won't look at me, is all over Johnny and every inane witticism he fires out.

Fast forward a couple of hours. Ruthie's long gone. Didn't even wait for the last DART. And myself and Johnny D are somewhere along Capel Street trying to figure out the next play of the evening. Funds are low. We're barely into term two and what little of my grant remains in the ATM will just about stretch to the next instalment of rent, like one of those either/or duvets that either covers your head or your toes. Johnny's tank is running on empty. Nothing beyond the shrapnel in his pocket, if the fecker can be believed.

There's meant to be a party out in Stoneybatter, some of the IT crowd. But you don't like to arrive out empty-handed and besides it's only recently gone midnight. You get to an IT party early, you end up having to talk to the earlybirds. And believe me, that's not something you'd risk twice. A scoop on the way, so. Maybe Sin É, or the Cobbler.

Jump cut to pub interior. 'Tell us this now, you,' goes Dowling, phlegming up into an accent that's more John B Keane than Ardal O'Hanlon. 'Would you say now, Maguire, that Ruth McArdle is hilarious now, would you say that?'

'Leave it go, Johnny, would you do that for me?' It's about his fifth time having a pop at her. Or at me would be nearer the mark. Bad enough that I have to stand the fucker another pint. But, of course, he doesn't let it go. Keeps circling about it, the way a tongue keeps touching on a sensitive tooth. And whether it's the pints or the hour or the supercilious eyebrows, or whether it's that I'm still mad at myself for crossing Ruthie, suddenly we're down on the floorboards, scrapping. Rolling over cigarette butts and sputum in a forest of truncated legs amidst which his glasses have gone skittering.

He's not much of a scrapper, Johnny. Almost at once my fingers are locking his jaw, his face all gargoyle and indignant. I'm digging my kneecaps hard into his shoulder joints. And as a dozen hands hoist me off him I taunt 'would you leave it go now, would you, now, you bollox?'

Where all that came out of I do not know.

The upshot, of course, not twenty minutes later I'm on my Jack Jones. He's skedaddled like a scalded thing, hands shaking so bad it took him two goes to pick up his glasses. Last words I hear, hoarse and high-pitched 'you really fucked up this time, Maguire.'

Yeah. Probably.

So I'm alone, somewhere down around Smithfield or the back of the Four Courts. Terra incognita, and not exactly friendly at this hour. Stoneybatter, I'm thinking. That party. Only I haven't picked up a takeout. Too bad I don't have my guitar with me, to bang out a few chords by way of a quid pro quo. My steps are being directed by some tentative internal compass. But the orange alleyway I've strayed into has the melancholy of a cul-de-sac. Not a sinner to be seen. Not so much as a cat.

By rights, I should just turn around. But no. The Imp of the Perverse, once again. 'Maybe,' she goads, 'there'll be a way through. It's just you can't see it yet.' So I persevere, each streetlight shrinking the shadow before me, then reeling it about until it's stretched into a Giacometti figure. There's no sound but my own reverberate footfall. I've been down this nightmare before.

End of the road. And sure enough, there it is – the opening.

It's a narrow passage, a solitary bollard thrust up from its jaw like a yellowed tusk. I even recognise the cavity down one side. Closed in by blind walls the laneway has an evil air. Brick and concrete brambled with graffiti. Bottle shards. A honk of cardboard and stale piss. I'm about halfway along when I hear the approach. A gravel voice speaking foreign. Shadows large and angular. Cue the zither music.

They've blocked the exit. One short, behatted. One huge as a bear. Making yours truly the eponymous Third Man.

The skinny one has a folded-up cane in the crook of one arm. Hook nose, eyelids closed but animated by the tiniest flutter. The tall one carries a huge accordion slung over one shoulder. Head as round and blank as a traffic beacon. Seeing me his mouth opens, a piano dropped down a flight of stairs. These guys, I'm thinking, have climbed out of the shallow end of the gene pool. 'Gentlemen,' I nod, making to pass.

The trouble, of course, the laneway is so god-awful narrow. At the best of times I'd have been hard pressed to negotiate the circumference of the giant with the accordion. Whether out of malice or ignorance, the foot-wide gap between instrument and wall is plugged by the blind man. A desiccated face, not without cunning. It's him I address.

'Do you mind?'

He does, it seems.

Why don't I turn round? Why don't I retrace my steps? It's not too late. There's nothing quite like sightless sockets to give you the willies. The grinning companion might've stepped straight out of a late Goya. So what's holding me? All I can think, the whole scene is glazed with the giddiness of the ludicrous. Not exactly hilarious. But yeah. Funny.

Could it be they haven't any English? Impossible to be certain in the fickle light, but there is a swarthiness about them. The snatch of language could've been anything – Romanian, Ukrainian, who knows, maybe even Shelta. Or Gaelic for that matter. But it wasn't as if my present intention wasn't blindingly obvious. Keep it light, I think. '*Scusi. Entschuldigung. ¡Por favor!*'

'You have maybe cigarette?'

A toll to pass. Seems fair. Only I don't smoke. All the same I go through that pantomime of tapping every pocket from coat to breast to trouser, which is doubly pointless seeing how the guy in charge can't see. The one who speaks. Sancho Panza's mouth is still flashing its keyboard missing a few keys. 'Look, gents, I'd love to parley ...' My instinct is to simply push on past. But you don't want to go laying hands on a man's accordion, especially not a giant's. And you can't just barge through a blind man like he was a saloon door. 'You after money? You're out of luck my friends. I'm a poor student. I haven't a kopek.' Which wasn't a mile off the god's honest.

'You think we are thiefs,' states the blind man, more in disgust than indignation. 'We are no thiefs.' And this has me wrong-footed entirely. I hadn't meant to insult the man. Even the BFG has shut the lid on his piano grin. I'm racking my brains. That accordion. That trilby on the small guy. He's in a cheap pinstripe, something out of the 1940s. The other's greatcoat, unbuttoned. Had we come across them one night, busking off Wicklow Street? That night we'd been upstairs in the International, the three of us. We'd gone to see *Huis Clos,* on Wee-klow Street (Ruthie's gag).

The way is still blocked. But I'm beginning to think that's out of carelessness. The blind guy can't see where he's standing, and the man-mountain is maybe too slow to realise his girth. All of a sudden I've a plan. 'Say, do you gentlemen want to come to a party?'

'A party?' Voice like a grating hinge.

'Sure! Maybe you could liven it up. Blast out a few tunes.'

His mouth turns down, as though he's literally chewing it over. 'A few tunes?'

'Only if you feel up to it. Hey, it's your call.'

'Where is this ... *party?*'

'Not far. You know Stoneybatter do you?'

The upshot, I set off with Little and Large. A few wrong turns. A few cocking ears at the debouchment of street and alley. It's a bizarre odyssey. Large is a dummy for all I know, and Little is not much given to talking. I make a few wry comments, try a couple of wisecracks. Neither gives any indication they're paying the slightest heed. At last we hear the low thrum, the smash of a bottle, the white noise of voices through an open door.

In the hallway my co-travellers are accosted by an anorexic with beard and glasses. Shane, I think his name is. It's his gaff. 'Look, Shane, they're with me. Ok?' He has a superior smirk you'd love to smack. '*Ok?*' He scans the hall for allies. *Whatever,* he shrugs, and subsides into the clamour of the living room. Tea lights. A fug of excess males. We make for the kitchen. It's more sparsely populated. A wincing fluorescent light, unpleasantly forensic. Carnage of dips and crisps. There's a punchbowl at low ebb in which wine-stained fruit tarnishes. I dribble the dregs into a trio of plastic cups, salvage a round of cheese and crackers. I even manage to bum a cigarette for Shorty.

The few hanging out in here are the social rejects, which is saying something.

Fast forward a couple of hours. Earlier I'd clocked Ruthie's plaid skirt and knee-high boots on the stairs, Toby Wilkins sitting real close in behind her, a guy I cannot abide. Arrogant individual. Essex. I'd melted back into the kitchen before she clocked me. When at last I made up my mind what I'd say to her *en passant* there was no sign of either of them. Not on the stairs, not in the front room. I'm hoping to Christ they've gone. The alternative, that they're in the bedroom beside the smaller one where all the coats are dumped, is too unpalatable. It has my gut clench up any time I can't distract it.

The party is beginning to thin. But the more it does, the more of a crowd precipitates into the kitchen. To hear the performers who, it turns out are Bosnians. Banja Luka. Been living here since things went crazy over there. When he's not rasping out lyrics like a beardless Ronnie Drew, Shorty plays something halfway between a kazoo and a harmonica which he cups in his hands. I do my best to pick out the bones of each Balkan chorus and parrot along. The crowd joins the merriment by clapping out the rhythm. Then, once in a way, the mood shifts. There's a lament, or a love song. The bear, it transpires, has as sweet a voice for harmonies as you could wish for. At such times Shorty leaves him get on with it.

Past four. Anorexic Shane is giving a look both smug and world weary. For my benefit, he makes a slow show of checking his watch. Which, of course, only encourages yours truly to keep the concert going. More and more riotously I wave my arms, cajole the listeners to join the raucous chorus, which they do. Syllables all zeds and vees which could mean anything. The bear is loving it, and waltzes his accordion about the kitchen. Each time we think it's over he kicks it off again, to a big laugh.

Then I clock Ruthie.

She's sat on a windowsill, having a good ole tête-à-tête with the blind man. Or she's listening to him, enrapt. Leaning in. A dark tale of his dark land, could be. How I lost my eyes. Or maybe not, the frown she has is light, almost amused.

No sign at all of the English prick.

I've picked up that she's picked up that I'm behind this intrusion of rowdiness into the party. And as she's leaving she fires me a look. One of those looks that goes on just that second longer than it needs to. Not quite Sally O'Brien, but near enough.

And I know I'm forgiven. And that is enough for me.

DISTANCING

As the call went on, the knot in Emily's gut tightened. She couldn't take the chance that Betty Beglin might simply hang up, smiling bemusedly (as Emily supposed), not knowing there was a deathly serious purpose to the call. She couldn't take the chance *he* might come back early.

But, of all things, Emily hated confrontation. Interaction of any kind made her apprehensive. Sometimes, approaching a hairdresser's or a shoe shop in the days when one could still do such things, she'd actually caught herself practicing in a low voice what she was going to ask for, as though she were back on her year abroad in France. A knock at the door or a ringing phone, and dread would turn a sudden somersault. Why could people not just text?

Betty Beglin could talk for Ireland. Her chatter had already dragged on so long Emily's latte was cold. Coffee had been a mistake. Her fingers, caffeine-quickened, were all a-jitter even as she'd dialled, so that it had taken two goes before she'd got the number right. But now that Betty had stopped banging on about whatever it was she'd been banging on about while Emily's innards were squirming like eels approaching a saucepan, the lengthening silence was ten times worse.

And at any moment Frankie really might return.

She looked out over Crossthwaite Park. No sign of him. No Joxer straining at the leash. She swallowed a dry dribble of saliva. 'I meant to ask,' she tried to compose her features to approximate facetiousness, 'how's that new au pair working out?'

'Toni? She's fab! The girls are crazy for her.'

Toni. *Antônia.* That was it! 'Yeah?' Her heart fluttered skyward, a lark startled from long grass. 'She's very *young*, no?'

'The company said she was eighteen. Yeah. I'm pretty sure, eighteen. Gi-*nor*-mous family back in São Paulo, eight or nine I think she told us, so she's well used to having bundles of youngsters pulling out of her the whole time. *A cambada,* she calls them. She's a scream, a real livewire. But honestly, she's been marvellous. I mean Shona I can understand. Shona takes to everyone. But Pauline? For the longest time they thought Pauline was,' her voice dropped to a confidential whisper, as though there might be an eavesdropper, '*on ... the ... spectrum.* Can you imagine, Pauline? She's shy, that's all. Shy! You know? I don't see why a child isn't allowed to be shy these days. But ever since Toni Oliveira arrived, she's a different kid. Right from the get-go she took to her. Of course, it helped that Shona took to her first. She often takes her lead from Shona. You see her English isn't great, I mean Toni's, but then I suppose that's what has her over here, to improve. I mean she's forever saying things like 'I didn't went'. You see? 'I didn't *went.*' It's kinda cute, really. And Shona thinks it's hilarious, but instead of getting annoyed about it, Toni sorta plays along. Makes a game of it. And then Pauline joins in, all giggles. I mean it's lovely to see her giggling away and spanking poor Antônia's behind. But really, she's marvellous. I can't praise her highly enough. And *George*! George is mad about her ...'

Had she stopped for breath once in all that paean, while Emily's breath had been shallow and rapid and ineffective? *George is mad about her*. Well that about said it all. 'But she must miss her home, no? Especially now, with all this ...'

'Oh god! Bra-*zil*!? You should just hear her on the subject of that *bobo* they have for a president over there. *Bobo*. That's what she calls him. I can't think of his name but she says he's like a Latino version of Trump. Get this! But without Trump's class! Ha! Ha!'

Emily took a breath. She took a slow, deep breath. She held it in till it hurt. Then she exhaled, entirely. Ok. Calmness. 'But wouldn't she have to be studying over here, isn't that the deal? Doesn't their visa depend on them studying here, too?'

'But that's just it! The language school has been marvellous. They run these online classes. Zoom, the same thing George is using for his conference calls. Look, Emily, I better leave you go. I have about a zillion things to be doing this morning ...'

Now or never. Say it! *Say* it, for Christ's sake. 'Betty. Look. Can I ask you something?' Heartbeat. Heartbeat. 'A ... *favour*?'

'Sure. Ya! What is it?'

'She, ahm.' Say it! 'She's walking around ...' say it, dammit! '... in these short little pants and, and a singlet. And no bra, like it was ... And with her belly on show for everyone to admire ...'

An unimpressed pause. A shift in the barometer. 'That's the Brazilians, Emily. They're like that. Every one I've met, anyway. They're young, god's sake! And the way the weather's been, well! Hasn't it been just *mar*-vellous? The Dublin Riviera, George calls it ...'

Knee-length boots? In a heatwave you don't wear knee-length boots! Not when you're eighteen. Now that she was stepping off the precipice, Emily's voice hardened. 'Then can you ask ... Antônia ... not to be hanging around Crossthwaite Park every evening? Couldn't she use, I dunno, the People's Park, or somewhere? It'd be a lot nearer to your place, for starters.'

A hostile static met Emily's request. Betty Beglin was just the type to take this for a social snub, whereas that was the last thing on Emily's mind. 'I mean it's ridiculous. It's not like any of them are social distancing. They're hanging around together like they were at Electric Picnic, or something ...'

'What's this about? What exactly has got up your nose, Emily? Toni has no more harm in her than any Irish girl her age.'

Now Emily was fired up. Annoyed. True, she was annoyed at her own lack of composure, her own lack of sleep in recent days as images and arguments tumbled like laundry through her mind throughout the small hours. But at least she was able to channel it now. Heart pounding, she took up the gauntlet. 'Well, she clearly doesn't know the first thing about social distancing. Yesterday evening, when Frankie was out walking Joxer, she stood there in her hot pants not two feet in front of him, never mind two meters. Flashing her teeth up at him. Big, bubbly laugh out of her, I could hear it though we're at the other side of the park. I even saw her squeeze Frankie's bicep.'

A stony silence. She could all but hear Betty Beglin's smile freeze to a Botox rictus. 'Emily, can I suggest, if you've a problem with Frankie talking to Toni then perhaps you should take it up with Frankie, no?'

A heart murmur. A trapped bird. 'Betty,' her voice scarcely there. 'Could you not just *ask* her?' Because she couldn't say it to Frankie. She daren't. '*Please?*' Not after what happened last time she'd reproached him for his free-and-easy manner. Not now, when he was fearing for his job, and tramped round the house all day like a caged animal.

'Emily. Ok. Listen to me.' Her tone had altered again. Another barometer shift. To something like concern. 'Has he ...?' Because Betty had seen. Last year. After he'd ...

'Emily, if Frank has said or, or ... *done* anything to you, you have to report ...' But Emily wasn't listening. The hall door had swung shut, shuddering the hall and banisters. The thud resounded like a gunshot through her chest cavity.

As Joxer's nails spilled like a hundred ball bearings across the parquet floor, as he blundered upward toward the mezzanine, Emily plunged the phone deep into her pocket. She clamped her eyes shut, inhaled, composed the smile to meet their return; the smile that, ever since the lockdown started, seemed only to put Frankie on edge.

First Time

First time I spoke to her?

You're not going to believe this. It was at the actual funeral, I swear to god. I realise how fucked up that must sound. Sorry, can I say that?

See, I'd never been all that close to Rudi. It's not as if he was in my class or anything. Course I knew him. You can't be on the same rugby team and not know all the guys, specially seeing how we got as far as the final of the Junior Cup last year, only to be beaten by Rock. But there's no disgrace in that, am I right? Sorry, I'm gone off the point. What I'm trying to say to you, I knew Rudi. But not well. He was the best tight-head Belvedere had had in years, whereas I'm a centre, which is a back. And like I say, we were in the same year, not in the same class. Not since senior school anyhow.

I was sad and all he died. More than sad. Shocked, like everyone was. I mean, it is shocking. Sixteen years of age, not even. You couldn't not feel it. But like I say, we hadn't been all that close.

So I knew next to nothing about the family. Or no. That's wrong. I did know about the sister. Bit of a looker. We'd all seen her in that Centra ad, you know the one? A smile to die for. Cheeky. You'd often hear the lads ribbing Rudi about her. Messing, like. In the showers. He was well able for them. She'd be a couple of years older, gone to uni over in Edinburgh or some place. So that would've put her well out of our league.

I don't know if you've ever been to a school funeral? I've been to three. I know, yeah. Hard to believe. Tell you one thing, they're proper weird, they are. Everyone smarted up. Any girls done up to the nines. Looking their best. Not like at a wedding or a debs, of course. Different vibe. Everyone is serious. Acting all solemn, which is another word for awkward. I guess everyone feels they're a bit of a fake, even the teachers. Like they're putting on an act, or.

Except those that were genuinely close to Rudi. A few of the forwards, he'd literally played with since Elements – that's, like, third class, yeah? Huge fellas now, built like brick shit-houses. I dunno, there always seems to be this bond where a pack's concerned. Maybe it's that their voices probably broke first. Or it's on account of how they've to learn to scrum. The real team effort required, see what I'm saying? Whereas with the backline there's always some fucker will never pass, always has to go on a solo run.

Sorry, I'm off the point again. But to see these big lads leaning on one another's shoulders, blubbering like little kids. That has to affect you. Because there's nothing as contagious as emotion.

One thing I've learned about funerals. Grief is ugly. Turns you inside out, it does. The sister was there in the school chapel, home from Edinburgh. And Rudi's girlfriend, who I knew to look at. She was flanked by a few of her pals. Alexandra girls. You had to feel for them, features all swollen and snotty with the crying. The sister, Zara her name is, like I say, she's a looker. A bit like Rudi was to be fair. But it's like her face was literally pulled inside-out.

Not the mother, though. I think that's what impressed me.

She's the only one kept the accent. Has that clipped way of speaking they have down there. *Frim Sith Ifrika*, Rudi used to do it, when he was messing. I mean the dad's from Dundalk originally, so he wasn't going to have an accent, or not that one anyhow. And Rudi was about two when they moved to Ireland, like. Zara would've been four or five.

She's what you'd call, I think, a handsome woman. Not a stunner like Zara, maybe, but you could see it wasn't off the stones that Zara'd licked it either. She was calm all through the speech. The eulogy, is that what they call it? Low-voiced. You could've literally heard a pin drop. A mother, like. It was down to her to speak on account of Zara was in rag order and there was no love lost between Rudi and his Da apparently. She stood there, on her own, elegant, dignified, speaking out to a crowd of adolescents about her only son – Ruud she called him – who'd literally dropped dead at training not three days since. You had to be impressed. I'm not saying anything, but I can guarantee you if that had've been my mother she would've been in bits, like.

After the speeches and everything, those of us from the Junior Cup team were supposed to line up and file past. Shake their hands. Commiserate. So you know the way you're supposed to say 'I'm sorry for your trouble', it's like this set formula? So I get as far as the mother, and her eyes look straight at me, I mean straight into mine like she's expecting something, and you know what comes out of me? 'Great speech.' I swear to. 'Great speech!' I could've literally fucking. Only you know what? Just for a second, and I mean literally a split second, I see this flutter on either side of her mouth. As if, despite everything, she's trying to fight down this smirk.

After that I don't know what got into me. I was.

Ah. Ok. I'm taking way too long to get to the point. To the business end. Am I right? I mean, that's what I'm here for, yeah?

Ok. I'll cut to the chase.

So after that, it got to where I was calling round regular. Doing odd jobs. The garden, mainly. All the stuff Rudi used to do about the place. All the summer holidays, I'd call round. She used to throw me a fiver anytime I'd cut the lawn; they had this old mower that was a bastard to start. Sometimes I'd catch her looking at me out the window. Only she'd have this faraway look, and I knew. I look nothing like him, but it wasn't me she was looking at. It was her son.

Of course, she had no way of knowing I hadn't been close to Rudi. None of his other pals was calling round, to see how they were making out. I'm not saying I blame them. I'm not saying that. They wouldn't have known what to say. I mean, what do you say? And then it might've looked suspicious, with the sister home from college and everything. I know my folks thought it was on account of Zara I'd started to take such an interest in doing their odd jobs. But Zara was away a lot of the time. She had her own life. And the Da? The odd time he was there you'd get this bang of drink off him. I couldn't tell you was that a new thing, on account of Rudi's death, like. But I've an idea things were strained in that house a long time before that.

So one day I'm doing the lawn, and the mower is acting up and cutting out every twenty yards, getting choked, and like I say it's a bastard to restart. And it's a hot day. I have my shirt open. And next thing she comes out with this jug of lemonade, homemade. Straight out of the fridge, ice cold. Delicious, it was. And then she goes 'why don't you take off your shirt? Ruud would've.' Just like that. Natural, no funny business. But I'm all embarrassed, and I kinda give her this goofy smile. I swear, ten minutes I'm standing there like a prize fuckin' eejit. Then she.

She puts her palm inside my shirt, onto my chest. Just like that. Right here, over the heart.

We go on standing there, and I can feel my heart pounding. It's like it wants to literally break out of the ribcage. But there's a stone wedged in my throat, so I can't even speak. Then after an age it's like she comes to all of a sudden. As if she's only just become aware it's me standing there. For a second she's puzzled, then it's as if a cloud passes over her face. She shudders, then she's gone.

All that week I can feel that palm on my bare skin like it's imprinted there.

The following Saturday there's no answer when I call round. But I've a gut feeling she's in. Not answering. So I go around the side – you can see into the kitchen – and sure enough there she is, sitting there at the table, still in her dressing gown, hair undone and with this hundred yard stare on her. I'd've been freaked out if I hadn't seen it before. She'd have it an odd time, when everything obviously got to her. I tapped on the window. She didn't so much as look up. All the same, I knew that she knew I was there.

The following week it was back to normal. Or as near to normal as we'd ever been. And then one day late August, about a week before I started back into school, I'm weeding the vegetable patch, and I can sense her presence. And when I look around, sure enough there on the lawn behind me are her bare feet, toenails painted and an ankle bracelet. She's watching me and smoking one of those cigarillo things she'd have an odd time. Only this time, whatever way her eyes are, I know it isn't Rudi she's watching. It's me.

To this day I don't know where I got the nerve. Ok, I can be a bit of a headbanger on the rugby pitch, but I've never been any use with girls. Rudi, now he was a natural flirt. Half the rugby team had permanent girlfriends, but I'd never so much as snogged a girl. Any dance or party, I'd bottle it. But there I was, and it was like I was literally watching myself standing up, going to her, taking the cigarillo from her hand, cupping her mouth and kissing her. I swear to you to this day I do not know where I got the balls.

Afterwards, when it was over – we'd gone upstairs – she sort of huddled up in a ball and started rocking herself, and I knew she was crying, this endless, bottomless crying, and all I could do was hug her from behind and just lie there, for an absolute age.

First time, that was.

I would love to know who dobbed us in. One of the neighbours, was it? Can you not?

It was hardly the Da. How would he have even known? I don't see why you can't tell me. Amn't I meant to be the victim here?

The *victim*. Look, I know what you're gonna say. You've explained it. It's not down to me to press charges. Or to drop them. It's up to the DPP if there's a case to answer. I'd only be called in as a witness, yeah?

All the same, Jesus. Defiling a minor? Are you guys serious?

What I'm trying to say, how can you say it was down to her? If anyone took unfair advantage it was me. You have to see that. I'm the one should be locked up. She was all over the place, like. One day up, the next day down. On the floor, man.

No one made me call round there all last summer. I knew exactly what I was doing. And I mean it's not like I'm a kid. I'm seventeen come February.

You can write that down, too. Otherwise there's no way I'm signing your statement for you.

ABOUT THE AUTHOR

David Butler is an award-winning novelist, poet, short story writer and playwright. His third novel, *City of Dis* (New Island), was shortlisted for the Kerry Group Irish Novel of the Year, 2015.

Fugitive (Arlen House, 2021) is his second short story collection. Butler's eleven poem cycle 'Blackrock Sequence', a Per Cent Literary Arts Commission, illustrated by his brother Jim, which won the World Illustrators Award in 2018, is the basis of his third poetry collection, *Liffey Sequence* (Doire, 2021).

Literary prizes for the short story include the Benedict Kiely, the Maria Edgeworth (twice), ITT/Red Line and Fish International awards. David tutors regularly at the Irish Writers Centre, Dublin, and is married to author Tanya Farrelly.